THE GALLOWS LAND

I heeled the horse forward, sitting slack in the saddle. Even traveling mostly by night, and even though it was not yet the middle of May, a man dries out in the desert, wearies bone-deep. I could understand now why my father had always called this kind of country "the gallows land"; unless you met it with strength and on its own terms, the way settlers must have done, it would kill you just as sure as a hangman's rope.

But the desert also had a way of dulling the mind, which was just the reason I had decided to ride alone through the Arizona badlands. I didn't want company or conversation because they would only lead to questions and then sharpened memories I did not care to dwell on. I had nothing, and I wanted nothing except to drift through the long days and longer nights until life took on some meaning again, if it ever would. . . .

THE GALLOWS LAND

Pronzini Bill

BERKLEY BOOKS, NEW YORK

This is a work of fiction. Names, characters, places, and incidents are either the product of the author's imagination or are used fictitiously, and any resemblance to actual persons, living or dead, business establishments, events, or locales is entirely coincidental.

THE GALLOWS LAND

A Berkley Book / published by arrangement with the author

PRINTING HISTORY
Walker and Company edition / 1983
Berkley edition / May 2001

The Penguin Putnam Inc. World Wide Web site address is http://www.penguinputnam.com

ISBN: 0-425-17957-5

BERKLEY®
Berkley Books are published by The Berkley Publishing Group, a division of Penguin Putnam Inc., 375 Hudson Street, New York, New York 10014.
BERKLEY and the "B" design are trademarks belonging to Penguin Putnam Inc.

PRINTED IN THE UNITED STATES OF AMERICA

10 9 8 7 6 5 4 3 2 1

THE
GALLOWS
LAND

CHAPTER 1

THE DAY WAS coming on dusk, the sky flame-streaked and the thick desert heat easing some, when I found the small hardscrabble ranch.

It lay nestled within a broad ring of bluffs and cactus-strewn hillocks. Crouched beside a draw leading between two of the bluffs was a pole-and-'dobe cabin and two weathered outbuildings. Even from where I sat my steeldust high above, I could see that whoever lived there was not having an easy time of it. Heat had parched and withered the corn and other vegetables in the cultivated patch along one side, and the spare buildings looked to be crumbling, like the powdering bones of animals long dead.

There were no horses or other livestock in the open corral near the cabin, no sign of life anywhere. Except for the wisps of chimney smoke rising pale and steady, the place had the look of abandonment. It was the smoke that had drawn me off El Camino Real del Diablo some minutes earlier; that and the fact that both my waterbags were near empty.

Most days there seemed to be a fair amount of traffic on the Devil's Highway—the only good road between Tucson and Yuma, part of the Gila Trail that connected California with points east to Texas. Over the past week I'd come on pioneers, freighters, drifters, a Butterfield stagecoach, a company of soldiers on its way to Fort Yuma, groups of men looking for work on the rail line the Southern Pacific had begun building eastward from the Colorado River the previous year, 1878. But today, when I needed water and would have paid dear for it, the road had been deserted.

It was my own fault that I was low on water. I could have filled the bags when I passed through the town of Maricopa Wells last night, but I'd decided to keep on without stopping; it had been late enough so that even the saloons were closed, and I saw no need to go knocking on someone's door at that hour. It was my intention to buy water at the next way station for the Butterfield line, but when I got there, close to noon, the stationmaster had refused me. His main spring had gone bad, he said, and they had precious little for their own needs. He'd let me stay there for most of the afternoon, waiting in the shade by the corral; not a soul had passed by the time I rode on again at five o'clock. And I had seen no one since, either.

I hoped the people who lived down below had enough water to spare. If they didn't I would have to go back to the Devil's Highway and do some more waiting; neither the horse nor I was fit enough for moving on without water. I could see the ranch's well set under a plank lean-to in the dusty yard and I licked at my parched lips. Well, I had nothing to lose by riding down and asking.

I heeled the horse forward, sitting slack in the saddle. Even traveling mostly by night, and even though it was not yet the middle of May, a man dries out in the desert, wearies bone-deep. I could understand now why my father had always called this kind of country "the gallows land"; unless you met it with strength and on its own terms, the way settlers like the ones below had to have done, it would kill you just as sure as a hangman's rope.

But the desert also had a way of dulling the mind, which was just the reason why I had decided to ride alone instead of traveling by coach through these Arizona badlands. I didn't want company or conversation because they would only lead to questions and then sharpened memories I did not care to dwell on. Memories that needed to be buried, the way I had buried Emma four months and six days ago in the sun-webbed ground outside Lordsburg.

People I knew there, friends, said the pain would go away after a while. All you had to do was to keep on living the best you could and time would help you forget—forget how she'd collapsed one evening after a dozen hours' hard toil on our own hardscrabble land, and how I'd thought it was just the ague because she'd been complaining of chest pains, and that terrible time when I came back from town with the doctor and found her lying in our bed so still and small, not breathing, gone. Heart failure, the doctor said. Twenty-eight years old, prime of life, and her good heart had betrayed her. . . .

Maybe they were right, the friends who'd given their advice. But four months and six days of living the best I could hadn't eased the grief inside me, not with everything and everyone in Lordsburg reminding me of Emma. So a week ago I had sold the farm, packed a few changes of clothing and some personal belongings and a spare pistol into my saddlebags, and set out west into Arizona Territory. I had no idea where I was going or what I would do when the three hundred and eighty dollars I carried in my boot dwindled away. I had nothing and I wanted nothing except to drift through the long days and longer nights until life took on some meaning again, if it ever would.

The trail leading down to the ranch was steep and switch-backed in places, and it took me the better part of twenty minutes to get to where the buildings were. The harsh daylight had softened by then and the tops of the bluffs seemed to have turned a reddish-purple color; the sky looked flushed now, instead of brassy the way it did at midday.

I rode slowly toward the cabin, keeping my hands up and in plain sight. Desert settlers, being as isolated as they were, would likely be mistrustful of leaned-down, dust-caked strangers. When I reached the front yard I drew rein. It was quiet there and I still wasn't able to make out sound or movement at any of the buildings. Beyond the vegetable patch, a sagging utility shed stood with a padlock on its door; the only other structure was a long pole-sided shelter at the rear of the empty corral. In back of the shed, rows of pulque cactus stood like sentinels in the hot, dry earth.

I looked at the well, running my tongue through the dryness inside my mouth. Then I eased the steel-dust half a rod closer to the cabin and called out, "Hello the house!"

Silence.

"Hello! Anybody home?"

There was more silence for a couple of seconds, and I was thinking of stepping down. But then a woman's voice said from inside, "What do you want here?" It was a young voice, husky, but dulled by something I couldn't identify. The door was closed and the front window was curtained in monk's cloth, but I sensed that the woman was standing by the window, watching me through the curtain folds.

"Don't be alarmed, ma'am," I said. "I was wondering if you could spare a little water. I'm near out."

She didn't answer. Silence settled again, and I began to get a vague feeling of something being wrong. It made me shift uncomfortably in the saddle.

"Ma'am?"

"I can't let you have much," she said finally.

"I'll pay for whatever you can spare."

"You won't need to pay."

"That's kind of you."

"You can step down if you like."

I put on a smile and swung off and slapped some of the fine powdery dust off my shirt and Levi's. The door opened a crack, but she didn't come out.

"My name is Jennifer Todd," she said from inside. "My husband and I own this ranch." She spoke the word "husband" as if it were a blasphemy.

"I'm Roy Boone," I said.

"Mr. Boone." And she opened the door and moved out into the fading light.

My smile vanished; I stared at her with my mouth coming open. She was no more than twenty, hair the color of near-ripe corn and piled in loose braids on top of her head, eyes brown and soft and wide—pretty eyes. But it wasn't any of this that caused me to stare as I did. It was the blue-black bruises on both sides of her face, the deep cut above her right brow, the swollen, mottled surface of her upper lip and her right temple.

"Jesus God!" I said. "Who did that to you, Mrs. Todd?"

"My husband. This morning, just before he left for Maricopa Wells."

"But *why?*"

"He was hung over," she said. "Pulque hung over. Mase is mean when he's sober and meaner when he's drunk, but when he's bad hung over he's the devil's own child."

"He's done this to you before?"

"More times than I can count."

"Maybe I've got no right to say this, but why don't you leave him? Mrs. Todd, a man who'd do a thing like this to a woman wouldn't hesitate to kill her if he was riled enough."

"I tried to leave him," she said. "I tried it three times. He came after me each time and brought me back here and beat me half crazy. A work animal's got sense enough to obey if it's whipped enough times."

I could feel anger inside me. I was thinking of Emma again, the love we'd had, the tenderness. Some men never knew or understood feelings like that; some men gave only one kind of pain, never felt the other kind deep inside them. They never realized what they had with a good woman. Or cared. Men like that—

Impulsively I put the rest of the thought into words. "A man like that ought to be shot dead for what he's done to you."

Something flickered in her eyes and she said, "If I had a gun, Mr. Boone, I expect I'd do just that thing—I'd shoot him, with no regrets. But there's only one rifle and one pistol, and Mase carries them with him during the day. At night he locks them up in the shed yonder."

It made me feel uneasy to hear a woman talking so casually about killing. I looked away from her, wondering if it was love or some other reason that made her marry this Mase Todd, somebody who kept her like a prisoner in a badlands valley, who beat her and tried to break her.

When I looked back at Mrs. Todd she smiled in a fleeting, humorless way. "I don't know what's the matter with me, telling you all my troubles. You've problems of your own, riding alone across the desert. Come inside. I've some stew on the fire and you can take an early supper with me if you like."

"Ma'am, I—"

"Mase won't be home until late tonight or tomorrow morning, if you're thinking of him."

"I wasn't, no. He doesn't worry me."

"You look tired and hungry," she said, "and we don't get many visitors out here. I've no one to talk to most days. I'd take it as a kindness if you'd accept."

I couldn't find a way to refuse her. I just nodded and let her show me inside the cabin.

It was filled with shadows and smelled of spiced jackrabbit stew and boiling coffee. The few pieces of furniture were handhewn, but whoever had made them—likely her husband—had done a poor, thoughtless job; none of the pieces looked as though it would last much longer. But the two rooms I saw were clean and straightened, and you could see that she'd done the best she could with what she had, that she'd tried to make a home out of it.

She lighted a mill lantern on the table to chase away some of the shadows. Then she said, "There's water in that basin by the hearth if you want to wash up. I'll fetch some drinking water from the well, and I'll see to your horse."

"You needn't bother yourself . . ."

"It's no bother."

She turned and went to the door, walking in a stiff, slow way but holding herself erect; her spirit wasn't broken yet. I watched her go out and shut the door behind her, and I thought: She's some woman. Most would be half-dead shells by now if they'd gone through what she has.

I crossed to the basin, washed with a cake of strong yellow soap. Mrs. Todd came back as I was drying off. She handed me a large gourd of water, and while I drank from it she unhooked a heavy iron kettle from a spit rod suspended above a banked fire. She spooned stew onto tin plates, poured coffee, set out a pan of fresh corn bread.

We ate mostly in silence. Despite what she'd said about not having anyone to talk to, she seemed not to want conversation. But there was something I needed to say, and when I was done eating I got it said.

"Mrs. Todd, you've been more than hospitable to share your food and water with me. I can't help feeling there must be something I can do for you."

"No, Mr. Boone. There's nothing you can do."

"Well, suppose I just stayed until your husband gets home, had a little talk with him—"

"That wouldn't be wise," she said. "If Mase comes home and finds a strange man, he wouldn't wait to ask who you are or why you're here. He'd make trouble for you, and afterward he'd make more trouble for me."

A foolish thought got itself into my head. "Well then, maybe I could—"

"I can't let you do that either, Mr. Boone."

"You know what I was going to say?"

"I think so. But it's my problem, not yours."

"There's no shame in taking help."

"I can't run away from him. I have no place to go."

"The West is full of places—good ones, better than this."

"You don't understand," she said. "If I let you take me away, Mase would just come after us. And he'd find us and bring me back, just like he did those other times."

"I might have something to say about that."

"You don't know him, Mr. Boone. He's crazy mean; he'd kill you."

"Maybe he would and maybe he wouldn't."

"He'd kill you," she said again. Her tone was soft and flat. "I know him and you don't. I couldn't stand to have a man's death on my conscience. No, Mr. Boone, it's better for both of us if you just leave, if you pretend you never even stopped here."

What could I do? It was her property, her life; I had no right to force myself on her. If she'd asked for help, that would have been another matter. But she'd made her position clear.

Outside, in the silky moon-washed black of early evening, I thanked her again and tried to offer her money for the food and water. But she wouldn't have any of it. She was too proud to take payment for hospitality. She insisted that I fill my waterbags from the well before riding out, so I lowered the wooden bucket on the windlass and did that.

We said our partings, and I swung onto the freshened steeldust and rode slowly out of the yard. But after I had gone fifty yards or so, I turned in the saddle to look back. She was still standing there by the well, looking after me, her hands down at her sides. In the silvery moonlight she had a forlorn, fixed appearance—as if she had somehow taken root in the desert soil.

CHAPTER 2

Two MILES SOUTHWEST of the Todd ranch, just off El Camino Real del Diablo, I noticed a circle of limestone rocks with a humped overhang on the near side. It seemed as good a place as any to make a short camp for supper. I'd rest a few hours after eating, I thought, and then ride on through the rest of the night.

I dismounted beside a dry-stream path angling upward into the circle of rocks. The path looked to be a runoff from a hollowed-out, natural water tank inside, but the tank itself was probably empty; there were no signs or markers to indicate otherwise. With my waterbags full, I saw no point in climbing up to find out.

When I had the steeldust hobbled I unknotted my bedroll from behind the cantle, took off the saddlebags and saddle. I hand-rubbed the dust off the horse's back, then gave him some of the grain I kept for him in a flour sack. After he'd eaten it, I poured just enough water into my hat to let him wash the dry grain out of his mouth.

The temperature had dropped sharply, the way it

does in the desert after dark. Dusty wind blew chill against my face as I moved over under the outcropping. I scooped out a shallow hole, gathered some ocotillo branches, and built a fire. With water from one my bags, I brewed a cup of coffee. And when I was done drinking it I made a place for my hips, spread out my bedroll, tamped shag tobacco into my corncob, and lay down with the blanket over me and my head on the saddle.

I smoked and looked up at the bright gold moon, the stars like bits of polished silver, and tried to make myself relax enough to sleep. But there was an odd uneasiness inside me, and the silence of the desert night seemed to hang heavy. That silence made me think of a dime novel I'd read once. In one of the chapters, some fellows were in the desert, and a band of Apaches was sneaking up on them. The hero was forewarned by the fact that it suddenly grew silent— no animal rustlings, no bird cries, just a breathless hush. Alerted by this, he and his comrades were able to drive off the Indians in true dime-novel fashion.

Well, that was just nonsense. The desert was always hushed at night; and not even one Indian, let alone a band of them, could move through it in total silence. It was when you heard sounds that you had to consider someone, or something, was coming your way. Eastern writers made that sort of mistake all the time. Whenever I came across one, it convinced me I could write better stories than the ones I read. Sometimes when I used to daydream, I fancied myself as a dime novelist; one who knew the lore of the country he wrote about and therefore wrote about it in a realistic manner.

But writing dime novels was just a dream for me. One I had had all my life; one I used now and then, these days, to help keep my mind off the pain of losing Emma. Tonight, though, it did me no good.

Tonight, for the first time in four months and six days, it was someone other than Emma who was disturbing my thoughts, who was responsible for that uneasiness inside me.

Jennifer Todd.

I kept trying to tell myself it was nothing more than a small nagging worry over her plight, the husband who drank pulque and beat her when he was bad hung over. Part of it was that, but there was something else, too. Something I could not quite get hold of.

Time passed and I still couldn't sleep. I sat up with my back toward the dying fire, started to tamp fresh tobacco into my pipe for another smoke. And then, like an echo in my mind, I heard some of the words Mrs. Todd had spoken to me at her ranch.

"If I had a gun, Mr. Boone, I expect I'd do just that thing—I'd shoot him, with no regrets. But there's only one rifle and one pistol, and Mase carries them with him during the day."

I listened to the echo of those words, and I thought about the way she'd been watching me inside the cabin when I first rode in, the way she'd suddenly opened the door and come outside. Why had she come out at all? Beaten the way she was, most women would have stayed in the privacy of the cabin rather than allow a stranger to see them that way. And why had she talked so freely about her husband, about the kind of man he was?

Then I heard other words she'd spoken—*"I'll fetch some drinking water from the well, and I'll see to your horse"*—and I knew the answer. I caught up my saddlebags, pulled open the straps on one, and groped inside.

My spare pistol was missing.

And along with it, a handful of cartridges.

I felt anxiety and a cut of anger. I couldn't blame

Mrs. Todd for what she'd done; it seemed she'd been
driven to it. But neither could I allow her to commit
cold-blooded murder with my weapon, not if I could
prevent it.

In a way, I felt responsible. Perhaps I hadn't planted
the idea in her head, but I had nourished it. I remembered my words to her outside the cabin: *"A man
like that ought to be shot dead for what he's done to
you."* If I permitted her to murder him, I felt the taint
of his blood would be on my hands as well.

There was another possibility, too—a worse one.
What if she was a poor shot? What if she missed
when she fired at him and he managed to overpower
her? He might just kill her instead.

I kicked off the blanket, scraped earth over the fire,
and gathered up my belongings. Then I saddled the
steeldust and rode hard back toward the Todd ranch.

The little valley was moon-shadowed, as solemn and
foreboding as a graveyard. From the trail above, I
could see the shapes of the pole-and-'dobe cabin and
the outbuildings; no lamplight showed anywhere. The
night hush down there was unbroken. The only sound
anywhere was the gentle stirring of the thin, cold wind.

I gigged the horse down the steep trail, hanging
onto the hope that Mase Todd hadn't yet come back
from Maricopa Wells. If she was alone, waiting there
in the dark for him, I might be able to talk sense to
her; I had offered her help before, and I would offer
it again. And one way or another, I'd get my pistol
back.

But it could be, too, that Mase Todd *had* returned
and she hadn't yet worked up sufficient courage to
use the pistol; that the two of them were in the cabin
together, sleeping. If that was the case, it would make
matters even more tense. I would have to try passing
myself off as a traveler seeking shelter, hope that Mrs.

Todd wouldn't give me away, and get her alone long enough to convince her of the daunciness of her plan. Either that, or take on her husband myself if he made trouble for me or her.

The third possibility, that he'd come and she had already shot him—or he'd done for her instead—I didn't let myself think about.

When I came to the foot of the trail I slowed the steeldust to a walk. He was blowing a little, making small sounds in the stillness; anyone awake in the cabin was likely to hear us coming. But the place stayed dark and quiet. There was still only the wind to hear, only the bulky shapes of the buildings to see— everything draped and hidden in shadowy black, like the dust-covered furniture in the house I had shared with Emma back in Lordsburg.

I looked over toward the corral and the little shed-like lean-to at the rear. There were no horses visible, but the lean-to had been built so that it faced away from the yard; an animal or two could have been sheltered underneath. I thought about detouring over there for a look, but it was a foolish idea. If Mase Todd was inside the cabin, he might hear me prowling, mistake me for a horse thief, and come out shooting.

The thing to do, I decided, was to ride slow into the yard, with my hands in plain sight, and hail the cabin when I got close to it—just as I'd done earlier today. Tension knotted the muscles in my back and shoulders; my mouth tasted dry. I hunched forward a little in the saddle, listening, watching the cabin door.

I was twenty yards from the cabin, ready to call out, when the shape seemed to materialize to my right, up ahead near the front wall; the words I'd been about to speak caught in my throat like dry biscuit crumbs. The shape was sprawled and twisted, covered in shadow so that I hadn't been able to make it out from a distance. Now that I saw it, a sick feeling roiled up in my stomach. And I knew I was too late.

It was a body—a man's body lying face down in the dust.

I swung down and ran to it. When I dropped to one knee I could see that his head was streaked with blood; it looked as though he'd been shot in the face. I put my fingers against the artery in his neck, to feel for a pulse, but it was a futile gesture. He was dead, all right.

I thought: Damn! and straightened up. The cabin was still dark, still wrapped in silence. "Mrs. Todd?" I called out. "You in there?"

No answer.

I went over and shoved at the door. It wasn't bolted or barred; it swung inward, creaking. I got the block of wooden matches out of my coat, broke one off, and scraped it alight on the adobe wall. The flare cut away enough of the blackness inside to show me the way to the table with the mill lantern on it. I crossed to there, used another match to light the wick.

The lamp filled the cabin with pale light. The room was deserted; so was what I could see of the bedroom beyond. Two of the chairs had been overturned, and there was a stain of soapy water where the washbasin had been knocked to the floor. There had been some kind of brief struggle in here, one that ended outside when Mrs. Todd shot her husband.

With my pistol, damn it, I thought. With *my* pistol.

I picked up the lamp and went into the bedroom. The lid of an old cedar chest stood open to one side, and two of the drawers in a rough-hewn dresser had been pulled partway out. A couple of articles of clothing were scattered on the floor. It didn't take much thinking to understand that Mrs. Todd had packed

some of her belongings, either before or after she'd
done her killing, and then ridden away from here.

She must have done it in a panic, I thought, because it was a foolish thing to do. If she'd stayed, or
at least gone to fetch the law in Maricopa Wells, she
could have claimed self-defense. By running, she was
as much as admitting to murder. The law would be
after her as soon as Mase Todd's body was found, and
even if they didn't find her right away, she would be
on the dodge the rest of her life.

I felt anger toward her, but there was sympathy
mixed up in it too. Foolish as she was, guilty as she
was, she was entitled to better than what she was letting herself in for—a second chance, an opportunity
to build a decent life with a decent man. It occurred
to me to go looking for her. If I could find her, maybe
I could make her listen to reason, bring her back to
face up to what she'd done before her husband's body
was found. . . .

But that would make me as dauncy as she was. I
had no idea where she'd gone; I could ride through
the gallows land for days without coming across her.
And even if I did find her and too much time had
passed, I could land myself in trouble with the law
as an accessory.

Let it be, I thought. What's done is done; she's
made her own bed and she'll have to lie in it.

And yet I couldn't get it out of my head that it
was my pistol she'd used to kill Mase Todd, that maybe
I had encouraged her to do it by the way I'd spoken
to her. It made me feel responsible again. I couldn't
just ride away and pretend none of this had happened.

Outside, from the direction of the corral, a horse
whickered faintly. The steeldust? He might have wandered over there, drawn by the smell of grain and
other animals. Or maybe there was another horse still
sheltered under the corral lean-to, a second horse—

Mrs. Todd's or her husband's—that she'd left behind when she rode out.

Or maybe she hadn't ridden out after all; maybe she was still here.

It was possible she'd been making ready to ride and spotted me coming down the trail, backlit by the moonlight. She would not have recognized me at the distance, and she might have stayed put under the lean-to, hidden, to watch and wait. At that same distance, I could have missed seeing any movements she made in the darkness.

Back in the main room, I blew out the lamp and set it on the table. The steeldust, I saw when I got outside, was over nosing around the well; the whickering hadn't come from him, then. And in that moment I heard it again, from the shadows back by the lean-to. I moved to the corral fence, along it toward the rear. When I got to where I could look under the lean-to I saw the other horse—a big roan, saddled, with a rifle jutting from the scabbard; he was standing placid near a watering trough, tied to one of the support poles. There was no movement in the heavy shadows back under the lean-to.

"Mrs. Todd? It's Roy Boone. If you're there, you'd best come out where we can talk."

Silence.

I let my hand drop to the butt of the holstered .44 on my hip. Maybe the roan belonged to Mase Todd and she'd taken another horse; but it made me edgy just the same. If she was hiding under there, there was no telling what she might do. She'd killed once tonight and she still had my spare pistol; she might take it into her head to cut loose at me, too.

"Mrs. Todd? Don't be frightened—I mean you no harm."

The wind made a faint keening sound and the roan whickered again, shuffling its hind legs; that was all.

I eased ahead to the back corner of the fence, where the rows of pulque cactus loomed black against the moonlit sky. From there, I could make out the rest of the space under the lean-to. There didn't seem to be anyone hidden in the shadows, but I moved around the corner of the fence, putting my back to the pulque cactus, and leaned over the top rail for a closer look.

The roan shied some when I did that, and the noise he made covered the sudden movement behind me. I heard it too late to do anything more than half turn, drag the .44 just clear of its holster. I had only a glimpse of the dark figure that came out from behind the nearest cactus, of the length of wood upraised in its hand. Then there was an eruption of pain in my head, in my right shoulder, and my legs buckled and I was on my knees, trying to lift the pistol with an arm that had gone as heavy as a blacksmith's anvil.

I never felt the second blow, the one that drove me all the way down into the dust and the blackness.

CHAPTER 3

IT WAS NEAR dawn when I regained consciousness. Pain lashed at me as I struggled up to my knees; my head was afire with it. There was a tingling numbness in my right arm, and I had trouble moving it at first. I used my left hand to explore my skull, felt a crusty scab of dried blood over one ear. The ear itself seemed swollen, and it hurt when I touched it.

I knelt there for a time, shaking with cold, rubbing my arm to get feeling back into it. The corral was empty now; the roan and Jennifer Todd were long gone. A few feet away, lying in the dust, was a cut length of pole about three feet long. Damn her, I thought groggily, she could have split my head wide open with a weapon like that.

Closer to me, within reach, was my .44; I picked it up and holstered it. Then I caught hold of one of the fence rails, used it to drag myself to my feet. Wobbly-legged, I made my way along the fence to the front of the corral. The steeldust was nowhere in sight, but the body of Mase Todd was still sprawled near the cabin door. And halfway between the corral and the well, my saddlebags and everything that had been in them lay scattered on the ground.

Mrs. Todd must have gone through the bags before riding out. Looking for money? She hadn't seemed that kind of woman, but then what did I know about her? She'd killed her husband, and she'd clubbed me senseless for no good reason; it didn't take much to imagine her as a thief, too. Well, she'd been frustrated in that respect, by God. There hadn't been any money in my saddlebags. Except for a five-dollar gold piece, all the cash I had was down in the toe of my boot; I could feel the wad of greenbacks tucked up against my toes. And the gold piece was still in the pocket of my Levi's.

But Jennifer Todd wasn't my main worry just now. If the steeldust had wandered off far enough so I couldn't find him, or if she'd led him off on purpose, then I was in a bad way. Even with El Camino Real del Diablo nearby, a man on foot in the desert wouldn't last long. And if anybody approached the ranch before I could get clear, I was likely to take the blame for Mase Todd's murder, no matter what I might say to the contrary.

I needn't have fretted about the steeldust, though. As soon as I went looking, I found him foraging in the vegetable patch on the far side of the cabin. Relieved, I led him back to the corral and tied him to one of the poles. Then I scooped up my scattered belongings, returned them to the saddlebags, and fastened the bags on the horse's flanks.

Daylight was coming on now, the sky pink-veined to the east; the air was already beginning to warm. I crossed to the well and hauled up a bucket of water on the windlass. Drank some to wash the dust out of my mouth and throat, doused my head with the rest. The cool water started me shivering again.

At the cabin, I paused for another look at what was

left of Mase Todd. He'd been a big man, with matted black hair that grew like fur on the backs of his arms and hands. She'd shot him in the face; the whole side of his head was gone. I didn't know what to do about him. Leave him where he lay, cover the body with a blanket to keep the scavenger birds and the direct sun off him? Or find a shovel and bury him somewhere? Burying him would be a kindness to Mrs. Todd, because if I did a careful job of it, it wasn't likely he would ever be found. But I was not feeling kindly toward her any longer, not after what she'd done to me last night. I would have to think on it some before I made up my mind.

The pain in my head was hellish, and it made thinking a chore. Perhaps there was something in the cabin, some sort of medicine I could use to ease the throbbing. I pushed the door open, started inside. And then stopped and stared.

The place had been ransacked, ripped apart.

Chairs and tables overturned, crocks of flour and sugar and other foodstuffs emptied and broken, pots and pans and utensils strewn about. In the bedroom, the dresser had been upended, clothing flung everywhere, the mattress on the bed slashed to tatters with a knife. The way it looked, all of that had been done in a frenzy.

I kept on standing there, feeling confused. Why would Mrs. Todd have done such a thing? Unless she'd gone berserk . . . but even then, why? And why hadn't she done it before I came, instead of waiting until after she'd used that club on me?

Somebody else, then? I thought.

Somebody who'd ridden in while I was unconscious, maybe? Or somebody who'd been here all along, who'd hidden out back of the corral when he saw me approaching?

It didn't have to have been Mrs. Todd who'd

clubbed me. All I'd glimpsed was a shape; it could have been anybody, a man as well as a woman. It didn't have to have been Mrs. Todd who'd searched my saddlebags, either.

But if that was it, it only confused matters more. Who was my attacker? What had he been looking for, to tear the cabin up this way?

And what had happened to Mrs. Todd?

I stayed in the cabin long enough to bind my head wound with a clean washcloth and to gather up a blanket from the bedroom. Outside again, I dropped the blanket over Mase Todd's body and then untied the steeldust. I led him around behind the corral, stopping on the way to pick up my hat.

There was nothing in the rows of cactus to tell me who had been there last night, but on the dusty ground beyond I found two sets of tracks. They led away from the ranch, through the greasewood-choked draw at the rear. One of the horses had a chipped shoe; that set of tracks overlaid the other set in some places, paralleled it in others. It didn't look as though two riders had left together, or that one rider had been leading the second animal. It looked as though the owner of the chipped-shoe horse had set out to follow the first set of tracks.

I led the steeldust into the draw. I had a burning curiosity to know just what had happened here last night; that, and the throbbing pain in my head, the anger that had built up inside me because of it, made me determined to find out.

I was halfway through the draw, following the tracks, when I heard the horses coming.

Sounds carry in the desert; the faint pound of hoofbeats was a long way off. Coming from the opposite end of the little valley, I thought, on the trail that led down from the direction of El Camino Real del Diablo. And not just a few riders—ten or more, judging from the rumble of the horses' hooves.

I couldn't see the trail or the ranch buildings from where I was, which meant that the riders couldn't see me, either. There was a chance that they had spotted me from above, before I entered the draw, but I doubted it was likely; the bluffs had been empty when I'd glanced up there. One thing was sure: I wasn't about to head back to the ranch to meet them. Not with that body lying in the yard, the cabin ransacked. For all I knew, those riders were friends of Mase Todd's. And in country like this, men tended to hold court on the spot, without listening to explanations. I had no desire to end my days on a makeshift gallows.

Mounting the steeldust, I rode the rest of the way through the draw at a walk; if I'd gone at a faster pace, the horse's hooves might have raised dust that could be seen from a distance. The ground began to slope upward, to break up into jumbles of rocks and scatters of catclaw and cholla. Ahead and above me, a formation of rock jutted from the top of a rise; from up there, I judged, you would have an unobstructed view back to the ranch.

I swung down, ground-reined the steeldust, and got my spyglass out of the saddlebag. The rumble of approaching horses was much louder now. I made my way upslope to the rock formation, keeping clear of clumps of catclaw, and hunkered down in the rocks' shadow. When I expanded the glass I could see both the cabin and the yard in front.

The riders were just coming into the yard—at least a dozen of them, as dust-caked as their mounts. They drew rein near the blanket-covered body of Mase Todd, sat their horses for a moment staring down at it. Then two of the men quickly dismounted. One of them, a bearish fellow with red hair poking out from beneath his hat and a bristly beard, ran to the cabin and threw open the door and disappeared inside. The other one, tall and lean, went over to the body. Sunlight glinted off the star he wore on the front of his shirt.

Lawman, I thought, probably the sheriff of Maricopa Wells.

And that made the group of riders a posse.

But I couldn't figure what they were doing at the ranch. Unless someone had reported the death of Mase Todd . . . Mrs. Todd? No, that made no sense. If she'd gone to Maricopa Wells to turn herself in to the law, the sheriff wouldn't have had cause to ride out here with a dozen men.

The others had dismounted now and stood grouped around behind the lawman as he peeled back the blanket, peered at the dead man's face.The redhead came out of the cabin, glanced down at the body, and then began making agitated gestures. Ignoring him, the sheriff draped the blanket over Mase Todd again and unfolded to his feet. Then he made a fanning movement with his hand and said something to the others. Two thirds of the men spread out over the yard, some moving toward the corral, some into the vegetable patch on the near side. The rest, with the redhead leading them, entered the cabin.

I closed the glass; I'd seen enough. It would not take long for the posse to find the tracks beyond the pulque cactus, and when they did they'd come through the draw. The longer I stayed in the vicinity, the worse my chances were of being seen.

I climbed down to the steeldust and swung into leather. I had a choice to make now: Keep on following the tracks, or veer off through the badlands and try to pick up El Camino Real del Diablo again. But it wasn't much of a choice. As much as I wanted to know where those tracks led, following them would keep the posse on my backtrail; and sooner or later they would spot me. There was no guarantee that I could follow the tracks anyway across the rough ground ahead. But if I veered off, that same rough ground would cover my own tracks and I could get to the Devil's Highway without pursuit. That way, I might never find out what had happened at the Todd ranch, or to Jennifer Todd—but neither was I likely to wind up with a noose around my neck for something I hadn't done.

I gigged the steeldust away from the tracks and up along the rocky slope.

CHAPTER 4

THE MORNING TURNED blinding hot as the sun rose toward its zenith, as I rode through a vast wasteland of eroded ridges and outcroppings broken only by cactus and occasional greasewood and mesquite. The mountains to the east seemed closer than they were, shimmering with heat haze. I passed a *playa,* a dry lake bed, glaring white under the sun from crusts of alkali and salts. Other *playas* seemed to appear and disappear in the distance—heat mirages that burned my eyes and fretted at my imagination.

No breeze stirred, not even the intimation of one. Nothing seemed to be moving except me and the steel-dust; even the snakes and lizards and scorpions had sought shelter for the day, to wait for the coolness of night to do their hunting. Once I saw, or thought I saw, a cloud of dust behind me; but it was a long way off, and it seemed to settle and blend into the haze. I was sure the posse hadn't picked up my trail.

There was still no sign of El Camino Real del Diablo ahead, but the angle of the sun told me I was pointed in the right direction, due south; and according to the map I carried, the road was more or less straight between Maricopa Wells and Yuma. The Devil's Highway had to be somewhere nearby. Once I reached it, I would be just another traveler on his way west.

I wondered if the tracks from the Todd ranch, had I stayed to follow them, would have led me to El Camino Real del Diablo somewhere farther on. Logic said it was likely. Along the main road there were water and way stations for the Butterfield Overland Mail, but out beyond it on either side there was nothing except more desert and probably a few other hardscrabble ranches. If Jennifer Todd had gone on the run, she'd want the Devil's Highway—not trackless desert, where Apaches roamed in small bands, and not any trails that led to her neighbors.

But had she made it as far as the road? Or had the owner of the chipped-shoe horse caught up with her? Or was *she* the owner of the chipped-shoe horse, she the one who had done the trailing? And if one or both of the two had reached El Camino Real del Diablo, in which direction had they gone? West, toward Yuma and the Colorado River? Or east, back to Maricopa Wells?

The questions kept irritating my mind, like cactus needles burrowed under a fingernail. But I couldn't think clearly on them, or on any of the other questions I had asked myself that morning. Between the heat and the thudding pain from my head wound, my thoughts rambled like those of a man on the edge of delirium. If I didn't raise the highway soon, I would have to find a place to make a shade camp. It would be pure craziness to keep on riding through the midday heat.

Near a shallow wash I drew rein and walked the steeldust into the shade cast by a clump of mesquite. I had a long drink from one of my waterbags, swung down, and gave the horse a shorter one from my hat. When I ran my hand across my forehead, the fingers came away dry. It was hot enough now to evaporate sweat as soon as it appeared.

Hunger pangs gnawed under my breastbone; I hadn't had anything to eat since camp last night, hadn't even thought of food until now. I took a piece of hardtack out of the saddlebag, and I was chewing on that when the steeldust let out a weary snort and flushed a couple of birds nesting behind a clump of ironwood inside the wash.

There was a flutter of wings, and the birds sailed up into the air over my head. Desert quail—Gambel's quail. I remembered a bit of desert lore my father had told me once, about that kind of bird. He had crossed the gallows land more than once, my old man—on his way to California to join the gold rush back in '49, home again to New Mexico after three years with enough dust to buy a ranch, back to Arizona Territory when a Texan named Jacob Snively discovered gold along the Colorado River in '58. My father knew the desert better than most.

Nature had decreed that Gambel's quail drank three times a day, he'd said. They always took to the air when they were on their way to water, and if you could keep them in sight, you could follow them to where that water was. After they drank their fill, they always walked instead of flew away, to conserve liquid by less effort. So if you saw them flying they were on their way to drink, and if you saw them walking they were already finished.

These quail flew southwest, toward where I figured El Camino Real del Diablo to be. I mounted up and rode after them. Water was a precious commodity out here, even at this time of year. A water tank would be a good place to make camp, too, particularly if it was close to the road.

I had gone no more than five hundred yards before I lost sight of the quail behind one of the bare, serrated ridges that rose from the desert floor. When I got around to the opposite side, they had disappeared. But from there, through the shimmers of heat, I thought I could see the highway stretched out in the distance. I couldn't be sure because of the haze and because there was another *playa* nearby, spotted with dust devils that undulated like Indians performing some weird ceremonial dance. The whole thing might have been a mirage.

The road was farther away than it seemed; a half hour of riding and we still hadn't reached it. But it was there, all right. A mirage shifts and evaporates after a while; the road remained substantial in my sight.

The steeldust was beginning to flag a little. I paused again in a patch of shade to let him blow and to give him a little more water, just enough to dampen his mouth and his insides. I couldn't afford to be generous with what little I had left, now that I no longer had the quail to show me where the nearest supply was. Besides, a horse had no sense when it came to water. As thirsty as the steeldust was, he would drink all I had in my bags, and enough on top of that to swell him, if he had the chance.

A mule was a much smarter animal. If you worked a mule all day in the hot sun, he wouldn't run to the water trough and bloat himself; he'd let himself cool, and when he was rested he'd drink a little, rest a bit more, and finish drinking when he was completely cooled down. It was the same thing with food. A mule ate what he needed; a horse was liable to overeat and founder himself. And it was the same thing with work, too. A horse would work until he keeled over from exhaustion, but a mule stopped when he was tired.

Thinking about the differences between a mule and

a horse made me think, in spite of myself, of Emma and our farm back in Lordsburg. And how it had been a joke between us that we were more like horses than mules.

After a hard day she would sometimes say, "You know, Roy, we should take a lesson from the mule."

And we'd laugh and I'd say, "One of these days maybe we will."

But we never did. It was just a joke between us. About how our mule was smarter than we were; how you'd never catch him working from before sunup to after sundown the way we did. We attacked each new day as if there were no tomorrow, and then one day, for Emma, there wasn't. I had not only worked myself like a horse, I'd let her work herself like one too. And it had killed her.

The memory of that, the pain of that, came back to haunt me every day. It was as if Emma's ghost were always with me, reminding me of what I'd done and what I'd lost. As much as I worried now about the heat, I found myself hoping it would grow even hotter—hot enough to burn those memories away again, if only for a little while.

It was coming on noon when we finally reached El Camino Real del Diablo. The road was deserted as far as I could see in either direction. I walked the steeldust along it to the west, scanning the desert on both sides for a suitable campsite. To the left, clusters of ocotillo, their thorny stalks reminiscent of bundles of sticks tied at the bottom, lined the road in regulated rows, as if they had been planted there by some sort of desert Johnny Appleseed. The terrain on both sides was the same as I had just ridden through: arches, pinnacles, natural bridges, basalt and sandstone shapes of every description—a nightmare blazing white and sere under that murderous sun.

I was still debating on a likely spot when move-

ment caught my eye near an oblique confusion of
eroded rock some fifty yards south of the trail. I
squinted, shading my eyes against the sun's glare. It
was a bird, a Gambel's quail; it came waddling out
into a patch of shade, raised its wings, and beat them
furiously. A second one joined it a moment later, then
the two of them skittered out of sight. I waited to see
if the birds would take wing, but they didn't.

I let heat-cracked lips stretch into a smile. I'd not
only found my campsite, but the way it looked, a water
tank as well.

Halfway to the rocks, the steeldust raised his head
and snorted; he had caught the smell of water. I had
to hold him back from breaking into a run. As we
neared the rocks I saw that they formed a horseshoe
pattern, and when we passed through the open end
we were at the edge of the tank—a hollowed-out
depression shaded by the walls of rock, full of
brackish-looking water like a miniature lake. Quail
scurried away at our approach; nothing else moved
that I could see.

A smoke tree grew off to one side, and I urged the
steeldust in that direction. The water smell was making him skittish. I swung out of the saddle, tied the
reins to the tree's gnarled trunk, and then gave him
some water from one of my bags to calm him down.
I didn't want him nuzzling into the tank until I had
made sure the water was safe. And I didn't want him
drinking more than a little until he'd cooled down.

The water was all right: sharp with the taste of
salts, but drinkable. What was left in my bags was
better; I would drink that first before I refilled them.
I ducked the upper half of my body in the tank to
ease my sunburned face, the heat rash prickling on
my neck. Not for long, though; the salts made my
head wound burn like hellfire.

I spent a couple of minutes checking the ground

and the rocks near the smoke tree, but there weren't any snakes that I could see. I unsaddled the steeldust, hand-rubbed the dust and lather off his back. By the time I'd finished, he had quit blowing. I led him down to the tank and let him drink until I judged he'd had enough. Then I fed him some grain, gave him a little more water to wash it down, and hobbled him.

When I finally sank down under the tree I was bone-tired and lethargic. With the tank to replenish my bags, I drained one of them and took some from the second. That was something else my father had told me about desert travel, something he'd learned from frontier soldiers who had in turn learned it from the Indians: It was better to saturate yourself with water whenever you could, because it helped ward off dehydration. A man could last much longer in the gallows land with a bellyful of water than he could if he kept sipping it at intervals.

It was too hot for a fire, too hot for cooking; I ate hardtack and jerky to appease my hunger. Too hot to smoke my pipe, too. I settled back against the tree trunk and closed my eyes. At least the shade cast by the rocks, by the blue-gray twigs on the thorny branches overhead, like billows of frozen smoke blotting out part of the hazy sky, kept it from being too hot to sleep. I dozed. And within minutes I was asleep.

The sound of rattling wheels and hoofbeats woke me.

I sat up, blinking. The heat was no longer intense, and the sky had begun to slowly change color, from brassy blue to a deep, almost grayish violet. Late afternoon, less than an hour to sunset; I had slept the better part of five hours. I felt some better for it, too. The ache in my head had lessened considerably, and my thoughts were clear again.

I stood, stretching stiffened joints, then went out through the open end of the horseshoe. A big freight wagon, drawn by a team of four horses, was rattling along the Devil's Highway, headed from Yuma toward Maricopa Wells. Neither the driver nor his companion on the high seat glanced in my direction, and I saw no reason to hail them.

The wagon clattered past. I stood watching it for a time, and as I did, two men on horseback appeared in the distance, coming from the east. When they reached the freight wagon they flagged it down, spent a minute or two talking to the two freighters. Then the men on horseback came riding on at a trot.

I didn't think much about them at first. I went back among the rocks, filled my waterbags, and saddled the steeldust. It was time for me to be riding on, too. Freshened as he was, and with night coming on, the steeldust could carry me another few miles toward Yuma before it was time to make camp for supper. There figured to be another stage line way station within twenty miles; I could replenish my waterbags again there, with any luck. Another three days or so and I would be in Yuma.

I let the steeldust have another drink from the tank, and I was just swinging into leather when I heard the horses approaching close by.

I rode ahead, out from the rocks. It was the two riders I had seen on the road minutes earlier; they had veered off and were coming at an easy pace toward the tank, both of them riding dusty roans. They were less than fifty yards away, close enough for me to get a clear look at their faces.

One of them was slightly built, with long, yellow hair like General Custer's. The other one was a big, bearded redhead—the same man who had been with the posse at the Todd ranch.

A cut of worry made me draw rein. They had seen me, too, and they slowed their mounts to a walk, warily, the way men will when they come sudden on a

stranger. But it couldn't be that they were after me;
this was far enough from the Todd place that I shouldn't
arouse any suspicion, and I was still sure I hadn't been
seen back there. They were probably familiar with the
terrain, knew that there was a water tank here; they
were only after that.

I lifted my hands to show them that I had friendly
intentions, started to call out a greeting.

And without warning, the yellow-haired man yelled
something I didn't catch, drew his pistol, spurred his
horse, and opened fire at me.

CHAPTER 5

THE FIRST TWO shots were wild; the third slashed by my ear as I ducked my head, jerked the steeldust hard to the left, and dug my bootheels into his flanks. It was reflex reaction, but even if I hadn't been taken by surprise, there was nothing else I could have done. I was no gunfighter; if I had stood my ground and tried to draw my own pistol, the yellow-haired man's bullets would have cut me down before I could have cleared leather.

I kicked the steeldust into a hard gallop, bent low over his neck. Another volley of shots sounded behind me, but none of the slugs came close. I kept my head down, scanning the terrain ahead through a sudden blur of sweat, the sound of the guns and the hammering of the steeldust's hooves loud in my ears.

Seventy or eighty yards to my left, an arroyo cut like a long, jagged scar through the desert floor; the arroyo ran in a more or less straight line for another hundred yards and then hooked diagonally in front of me and off to the right. When I cleared the rocks where the water tank was, I could see that the terrain on the other side was rumpled and heavily grown with cholla and catclaw. The cactus and the rough ground extended right up to where the arroyo sliced through into open desert beyond.

I swiveled my head without raising up in the saddle. The two men were coming on hard behind me, not more than thirty yards distant. They weren't doing any more shooting now; firing a handgun from the back of a running horse was a tricky business at best, and the fading daylight and spumes of dust kicked up the steeldust's hooves blurred the distance between them and me.

The wound over my ear spasmed with pain as I twisted my head to the front again. I knew I couldn't outrun them up here, even though the steeldust had to be fresher than their mounts. The terrain was too rugged and the cactus too treacherous; cholla spines were needle-sharp and seemed to jump into the flesh as soon as they were touched. The steeldust would cripple up, panic, and pitch both of us down before we got ten yards.

There was no place ahead where I could make a stand. And if I drew rein and wheeled around to fight them in the open, it was two guns against one; the odds were all in their favor. The only chance I had was the arroyo. If I could get down into it, and if the floor was passable, I might be able to outdistance them that way. Or at least find some cover to try standing them off.

The steeldust stumbled as I veered him toward the arroyo's rim, and for a second I thought his forelegs were going to buckle. As it was, he blew hard through vented nostrils and tried to quit running. I kicked him out of that, got him pointed again. Dust choked my lungs, started me coughing. I ducked my head against the sleeve of my shirt to clear the sweat out of my eyes.

We were near the arroyo now, running parallel to its edge. It was maybe a hundred yards wide at this point, a good forty feet deep, with steep, layered shale walls extending away on both sides. Boulders and ironwood and mesquite littered its sandy bed, but as far as I could see, it was passable. The walls were too sheer here for the steeldust to scale them without losing his footing, but up ahead there was a cut where part of the near wall had eroded away and formed a gravelly slide. I would have to slow the horse to take him down there; he'd balk for sure if I tried to do it on the run.

I threw another look over my shoulder, saw that I hadn't gained any ground on the two men. Twenty feet from the cut, I brought the steeldust up and neck-reined him toward it. I had to straighten in the saddle to do that, and a second later I heard a cracking sound behind me—another wild shot. The muscles along my back rippled with tension. But I kept my eyes on the slide and the bed of the arroyo below, fighting the steeldust into the cut.

He stumbled again when his forelegs hit the loose gravel, then reared back to keep his footing. I reared back with him, and the gun cracked once more behind me; this time the bullet made a whining ricochet off a piece of shale close by. I kept my body straight in the saddle as the steeldust half plunged, half slid down the incline. Then his front hooves clicked on solid stone and he lurched forward out of the gravel, snorting. I laid myself across his neck again as we charged ahead through clumps of mesquite on the sandy bed.

The horse couldn't run down here because of the boulders and the broken pieces of shale scattered among the desert growth; I had to take him ahead at an awkward trot. When we came around a man-sized boulder I looked back. The two of them were just

coming up to the cut, the redhead in the lead. But he
didn't push his horse onto the gravel slide; he drew
rein, shouted something to the yellow-haired man, and
dragged his rifle out of the saddle scabbard. The other
one followed suit. Then I saw them spur their mounts
along the rim of the arroyo, and I realized the mistake I'd made. They weren't going to keep on giving
chase; they were going to try to pick me off from up
above.

A feeling of panic rose in me. I fought it down,
gigged the steeldust around another boulder and
through a patch of ironwood shrubs. Up ahead, the
arroyo began its hook to the south. I couldn't see what
lay beyond the turning until I was into it—and then
I brought the steeldust up sharply, and the sweat on
my body seemed to turn to ice.

The entire width of the arroyo was blocked by boulders, huge jagged chunks of shale, the shattered remains of smoke trees and other vegetation. A flash
flood had raged through the wash at some point, collapsed both walls, and left tons of debris in its wake.
There was no way I could take the steeldust through
or over that barrier. And without the horse, trying to
get clear on foot, I had no chance at all.

Trapped.

The panic flared again, drove me out of the saddle. Up above, I saw the two men rein in; they'd seen
the blockage too. The redhead lifted his rifle, squeezed
off a shot. But I was already running by then, crouched
low, hanging onto the steeldust's reins, and the bullet
missed wide, kicked up a spout of sand near one of
the horse's hind legs.

He reared in fright, tried to full free; I managed to
drag him to cover behind a boulder. Two more shots
echoed in the early-evening stillness, both bullets
spanging harmlessly into the rock. I tied the reins to
an outcropping, hobbled the steeldust to keep him from

plunging, from pulling loose and bolting; they'd shoot him first thing if he broke clear. Then I drew my pistol and eased around the boulder, hunkered low, to where I could look up along the arroyo wall.

The two men were out of sight now. That could mean they'd taken their horses back away from the rim to picket them and that they'd fan out and come back on foot with their rifles. Or it could mean they were riding back to the cut and that they'd come at me through the arroyo. Or it could mean both: one of them staying up there with a rifle, the other one looping back into the wash. Or, worst of all, one could sit up on that side while the other maneuvered around the arroyo back near the water tank and came up on the opposite bank; if they worked it that way, they could put me in the middle of a crossfire. I had no way of telling which it was going to be until they showed themselves again, and then it might be too late.

But even though things looked bad, the fear had eased in me and was being replaced by a slow buildup of anger. Once, during the War Between the States when I'd served in the Union Army, I'd been part of a patrol that had been ambushed by a Rebel unit, and we'd been pinned down under heavy fire for eighteen hours before reinforcements came. Anger had replaced my initial panic then, too, and it had kept me clearheaded throughout the skirmish; a couple of other volunteers had given in to their fear and died as a result. A crisis brought out the best or the worst in a man. The best had come out in me that day fifteen years ago in Virginia; the same would have to happen here if I was going to survive.

I moved farther back behind the boulder and scanned the area. I didn't want to stay where I was, where they'd last seen me; while I had the chance I had to try to get as far back along the arroyo as I could before either or both of them reappeared.

The steeldust had gentled down. I untied and un-hobbled him, checked the bank again, and then led the horse quickly and as silently as possible away from the boulder. Twenty yards distant, over toward the near bank, there was a long jumble of rocks high enough to shield both me and the steeldust from above. I took him into their shadow, walked him to where the rocks petered out in a patch of mesquite. Without letting go of the reins, I peered around and up toward the bank.

This time, something was moving up there.

I tensed, squinting in the dusky light. One man, down on his belly, crawling to where a small out-cropping jutted near the edge—the yellow-haired one. I watched him slither up behind the rock, saw the bar-rel of his rifle poke out. Nothing happened for a few seconds; then he squeezed off three shots in succes-sion, spraying the bullets around the boulder where I'd been before. He hadn't seen me move and he didn't see me where I was now, a good thirty yards back along the wash; otherwise he wouldn't have opened up on the boulder. It could be he was trying to get me to return the fire so he would know if I was still there, but more likely he wanted me to know where *he* was—keep me busy while the redhead came at me from a different direction.

I stood motionless, watching. He didn't fire again. But I could still see the barrel of his rifle poked out from behind the rock.

Where was the redhead? If he'd come down into the arroyo, I stood a fair chance. But if he'd looped around and was approaching on the bank above me . . .

The sun was gone now and the sky was a smoky color shot through with streaks of crimson. Shadows lengthened and deepened among the rocks and shrubs along the wash. Night came down fast in the desert;

it would be full dark in another few minutes. The darkness would be in my favor, but not so much that I could hope to escape under its blanket. The moon was already up, fat and gibbous: There would be plenty enough light to see by and to shoot by.

Quietly I moved back to the steeldust and swung up onto his back, keeping my body low over his neck so that I wouldn't be visible above the rocks. He shuffled a little in the sandy earth, but I leaned forward and rubbed his muzzle to keep him still. Then I eased him over against the rocks, extended my body so that I could look around the far edge of the last one in line. Its configuration was such that I could watch the bank and still keep the steeldust's head hidden below.

Minutes passed. The man behind the outcropping stayed where he was, not using his rifle, waiting as I was. Good horse that he was, the steeldust remained placid. The crimson streaks faded out of the sky and it turned from smoky gray into a deep purplish-black. A faint glow lingered on the horizon, prolonging the twilight. Nothing moved anywhere that I could see. And there were no sounds in the heavy stillness of dusk.

Waiting, tense and watchful in the saddle, I wondered for the first time why the two men had opened fire on me. It was possible that the two of them were outlaws and that their intention had been and still was to rob me; but the redhead had been with the posse this morning, and it wasn't likely that an outlaw would be riding with the sheriff of Maricopa Wells. And it had been the yellow-haired one who'd first opened fire on me. Did they suspect me of Mase Todd's murder? If this had happened back in the valley, the gunplay would have made sense; but I was reasonably certain I hadn't been seen, and out here on the desert, miles from the Todd ranch, I was just another stranger passing through. Why would they take me as Todd's killer? And if they hadn't taken me that way, why shoot at all?

Night wrapped itself around me as I worried the questions through my mind. Drenched in moonlight, the arroyo walls and eroded formations of rock took on a ghostly, other-world look. Overhead, stars burned in the silken black. The night wind came up, blowing first cool and then cold, drying the sweat on my body and putting a chill between my shoulder blades. With the first venturings of night creatures, the stillness was less acute now; an owl cried out in silhouette against the moon, a coyote bayed a long way off.

Then, finally, I heard something else, the kind of sound I had been straining to hear—a faint scraping among the shadows farther down the wash.

It might have been a snake or a small animal, but it had sounded like a bootsole rubbing through sand or against rock. I held my breath, leaning forward again to stroke the steeldust's muzzle so he wouldn't make any noise and give away my position. The sound did not come again, but after several seconds I saw movement over near the opposite bank—one shadow detaching itself from another behind an ironwood shrub. An instant after that, the dark shape of a man glided across a patch of moonlit earth, Indian-quiet, and immediately disappeared behind an outcropping.

The stillness held for another four or five seconds. Then the rifle up on the bank shattered it, sent a pair of bullets toward the boulder where I'd hidden earlier. The steeldust made a skittish movement, but the sound was lost in the echoing ring of the shots. Another volley followed the first two. None of the slugs sang off the boulder; it seemed the yellow-haired man was shooting high, into the opposite wall.

Now I knew just what they were up to. The one with the rifle was supposed to keep me pinned down while the redhead worked his way on foot at a back angle toward the boulder for a killing shot. In the moonlight, the yellow-haired man could see the red-head moving along the arroyo, and when the big one got close enough, he'd opened fire. He was shooting high so that he wouldn't risk a ricochet picking off his partner.

This was my chance, maybe the only chance I'd have. I flexed my fingers around the grip of my .44, holding the steeldust steady, watching the outcropping where the redhead had vanished. It was maybe a dozen yards from my hiding place, and the ground between was clear of stone and broken hunks of shale. I couldn't see the cut where I'd come down into the wash, but I judged it to be no more than twenty yards beyond the outcropping, hidden by the shadows and by intervening rocks and shrubs.

The shooting had stopped briefly. When it started again, the redhead came out from behind the outcropping and made his run toward the next nearest place of concealment—a triangular slab of shale jutting at an angle from the base of the far wall, maybe thirty feet away. From there he would be able to see that there was no one behind the boulder, but I did not let him get that far. He was a little better than halfway to it when I made my move.

I jerked the steeldust away from the rocks, heeled him hard, and sent him pounding out onto the open section of the bed. The sudden movement brought the man over there wheeling around in surprise. I fired twice at him before he could set himself; both shots were wild, but they accomplished what I'd intended them to. He threw himself to the ground and scrambled for cover behind the shale slab.

The steeldust was through the open stretch of ground and into the shadows behind another good-sized boulder before the man on the bank realized what had happened and got his rifle turned in my direction. I heard his first shot slash through ironwood branches off on my left, the second keen off rock somewhere behind me. Then I was out to where I could see, outlined in the moonlight a few yards ahead, the gravelly slide and the wall cut above.

I kicked the horse onto the incline, eased up on the reins for the surge upward. His hooves churned the loose shale, creating a small avalanche, but he kept his footing and his momentum. The man down in the wash had started to yell; the words were lost in another crack from the rifle just as the steeldust plunged through the cut onto solid ground above. The yellow-haired man was down on one knee at the edge of the wash, the weapon butted to his shoulder; I saw the muzzle flash again, but he hurried that shot, too, and the bullet missed wide.

To my left across thirty yards of open ground, but closer to me than to the yellow-haired man, their horses were picketed at a cluster of ocotillo. As soon as I saw them, I made an instantaneous decision. If I turned to the south and ran for El Camino Real del Diablo, they'd be mounted and in pursuit within minutes; and with the bright moonlight, I might not be able to outrun them or elude them. I took the immediate risk instead, still gambling on the element of surprise: I flattened out across the steeldust's neck, leaned to the right away from the man with the rifle, and reined the steeldust hard toward the other horses.

When the yellow-haired man realized what I was doing, he hurried his next shot and missed again. Then he made the mistake of levering up and trying to run for the horses. By then I was less than thirty yards from where they were picketed. I raised up and fired twice over the animals' heads, shouting at the top of my voice. Both horses reared in fright. I fired again, saw first one and then the other break loose from the dry ocotillo limbs.

I neck-reined the steeldust away from them, back to the south, then let up on the reins and gave him his head. The other two horses came charging along behind. The rifle hammered once more, and when the echo died away I heard another shout go up. I swung my head around and looked back. The man in the wash was just scrambling up through the cut; the yellow-haired man was down on one knee again, but he didn't do any more shooting. Either he was out of ammunition or he didn't want to risk hitting one of their horses.

It was over.

But I stayed low in the saddle and I didn't slow the steeldust to let him blow until we were on the Devil's Highway and pointed toward Yuma. The other horses quit their panicked run at the same time, fell behind, and drifted off in different directions. It would take those two hardcases hours to track them down, maybe all night. The way I felt just then, I hoped they wouldn't find them at all.

CHAPTER 6

I RODE EL Camino Real del Diablo for three hours, keeping a steady pace, stopping only once to water the steeldust; I wanted to put plenty of distance between me and those two men before I made a short camp and rested for a while. The road was deserted and except for a platoon of soldiers camped alongside a dry stream bed, I had the night to myself. The fire in the soldiers' camp looked inviting—the night wind was chill and I could have used a cup of hot coffee—but I was in no mood for company or conversation. I passed it by without a second glance.

Near midnight, I was tired enough and cold enough to start hunting for a campsite. I found one before long, under the overhang of an arched sandstone ledge that faced away from the road. When I had the steeldust hobbled and unsaddled and fed, I built a fire with ocotillo branches. The heat from that and from two cups of steaming coffee warmed me and took some of the stiffness out of my joints. But my head still ached, and the tension that had built up in me during the near-fatal skirmish with the redhead and his partner still lingered.

The anger lingered, too. I had been badly used on two occasions now and I did not know why or, except for Jennifer Todd, by whom. But other than the two hardcases, and maybe the sheriff of Maricopa Wells, the only person who could answer the questions that tumbled through my mind was Mrs. Todd herself, and I had no idea where she was or how to find her. Like it or not, my only choice was to swallow this day's indignities, as I had swallowed those of last night, and keep on riding west. The sooner I got clear of the gallows land, put all this trouble behind me, the better off I would be.

I wrapped myself in the blanket from my bedroll, smoked a pipe, and then lay down close to the fire with my pistol unholstered at my side. After all that had happened the past twenty-four hours, I was not about to take my safety or anything else for granted.

Sleep came hard. To keep from fretting about Jennifer Todd and my brush with death, I tried to think about the future, about finding a new life somewhere, in California or in the Northwest; settling down again, on land that grew tall, green grass and shade trees instead of hardscrabble vegetation and poor graze; maybe even writing again—dime novels, or something better. But there was no comfort now in any of that. Trying to mold an image of the future was nigh impossible when the present was unsettled and the past filled me with such pain and yearning. Most of my dreams had already been shattered, and the ones that were left seemed empty and insubstantial. They held no more real promise than that powdery soil Emma and I had tried so long to farm.

When sleep finally came it was fitful and plagued by vague nightmares. I awoke gritty-eyed and unrested. It was still dark, and when I lit a match to

check the face of my pocket watch I saw that it was
almost four o'clock. I ate some hardtack, washing it
down with lukewarm coffee, then saddled the steeldust and set out again toward Yuma.

An hour before daybreak, I came on another way
station for the Butterfield stage line. But I saw no
reason to stop, and I passed it by. At the first silvery
light of dawn, a string of heavily laden freight wagons, probably bound for Tucson, clattered by; and
later, after the sun rose between distant mountain
crests, I passed a rutted trail that wound off northwest through dry-rock hills and eventually led to a
place called Dent's Landing, according to a sign at
the fork. I saw no one other than the men on the
freight wagons, no sign of the posse from Maricopa
Wells or of the redhead and his yellow-haired side-
kick.

I rode on through the heat of early morning. The
wind was still up, hot and dry by then, and it blew
a fine film of dust into my face; I had to mask
myself with a bandanna for protection. By eleven
o'clock the heat was intense. The sun burned my neck,
set the wound over my ear to throbbing again. My
eyes began to ache, to play tricks on me; mirages appeared and disappeared like phantoms at the edge of
my vision. The steeldust was starting to flag, too. It
would be foolish to keep on pushing him, even at the
slow pace we were traveling, through the savage heat
of noonday and early afternoon.

I made camp again, in the shade of an oblique
confusion of lava rocks. One of my waterbags was
already empty, and after I watered the horse and myself, the other one was less than half full. But I wasn't
worried about that. There figured to be another way
station not far ahead, and I could fill the bags when
I reached it.

I slept easier this time, despite the heat; the desert

ṣun had dulled my thoughts, dried me out like a piece of old leather. It was four-thirty and some cooler when I awoke, and I felt rested again. I gave the steeldust some grain and water, and within a half hour we were back on El Camino Real del Diablo.

Just short of sundown, I came on the next way station. Like the others along the Devil's Highway, it was a cluster of adobe buildings grouped alongside the road—the main building that housed the stationmaster's quarters and travelers' accommodations, an eating house, a bunkhouse for the hostlers who worked there, and a pole corral and animal shelter. A pair of Mexicans in straw sombreros were shoveling manure near the shelter; they stopped working and watched me warily as I rode up. So did the old man with cotton-colored hair and whiskers sitting in a home-made chair in front of the main building, a harness he was mending draped over his knees.

A shotgun leaned against the wall behind the old man, and he tilted his chair back so that his hand was close to it as I drew rein. A cud of tobacco bulged one of his leathery cheeks; he moved his head to one side to spit, but his eyes never left me. Apache raiding parties were the main hazards to the men who ran these stage stops, but outlaws and grifters were other hazards. Any stranger on horseback was suspect until he proved his intentions.

"Evening," he said, and waited.

"Evening, sir. All right if I step down?"

"Depends on what's on your mind."

"Water to fill my bags and a hot meal is all."

"Water's scarce out here. Can you pay?"

"Yes, sir."

He nodded. "Hot meal's a dollar. Unless you take a night's lodging; then it's fifty cents."

I hadn't considered spending the night here, but now that I did, it seemed like a reasonable idea. The

steeldust could use some care and fresh grain, and
even though I was rested, I still felt stiff from the
long hours in the saddle and from the hard ground
I'd been sleeping on; it would be good to spend a
few hours stretched out on a bunk. And I could be
up and on my way well before daybreak tomorrow.

"How much for the night's lodging?" I asked.

"Two dollars. Fifty cents extra to board your horse."

Those were steep prices, but out here in the desert,
you had to pay for your privileges. I said, "Fair
enough. I'll stay the night if you'll have me."

"Cash in advance," he said. "Butterfield company
policy."

"Yes, sir."

"Step down, then."

I dismounted, took off my hat, and rubbed at the
cake of dust on my face. Watching me, the old man's
eyes narrowed.

"What happened to your head?"

Gingerly, I reached up to touch the washcloth bandage. "I took a fall," I said. "Nothing serious."

He didn't say anything. I got the five-dollar gold
piece out of the pocket of my Levi's and went over
and handed it to him. He looked it over, as if he
thought it might be counterfeit, and then nodded again
and said, "Two dollars to fill your waterbags. This'll
cover everything."

I gave him no argument. That seemed to relax him;
he smiled faintly, showing store-bought teeth, and
dropped the gold piece into his shirt pocket. Then he
spat again and got to his feet. His eyes were friendlier now.

"Looks like you been on the road a while," he
said. "Come far?"

"Lordsburg, by way of Tucson."

"Alone across the badlands?"

"Yes, sir."

"Where you headed?"

"Yuma. Then California, maybe; I'm not sure yet."

"Just drifting?"

"That's right." And for some reason, some quirk of my mind, I added, "My wife died a few months back, in Lordsburg."

The hard, grizzled lines of his face softened somewhat. In a different tone of voice he said, "Sorry to hear that, son. Natural, was it?"

"Natural."

"The good die young, I reckon." He shook his head. "My name's Rhodes, Frank Rhodes. Stationmaster here."

"Roy Boone."

He gave me his hand, and I took it. "You can wash up inside," he said. "I'll show you where you'll bunk."

"Much obliged."

Rhodes moved away from me and yelled over at the shelter, "Esteban!" One of the Mexican hostlers climbed over the corral fence and came toward us. I took the saddlebags off the steeldust's flanks, turned the horse over to Esteban, and then followed Rhodes inside the station.

The main room was fair-sized, ocotillo branches laid on the fireplace hearth but not yet burning, a scattering of tables and benches. A coal-oil lantern burned on one of the tables, and on a bench near the door were a pannikin of water and a side dish of soap. He picked up the pannikin and soap, led me through a doorway on the left and into a room that contained two bunks and a roped bedstead.

"Supper in the eating house yonder when you're ready," he said and left me alone.

On top of the bedstead was a bedtick stuffed with grass and covered with an old Indian blanket; I laid my saddlebags over the foot of it. I washed my face and hands, unwrapped the bandage over my ear, and dabbed at the wound underneath. It was scabbed and healing; I didn't bother to rebandage it. Then I got my razor out and used it and a cracked mirror to scrape off three days' growth of beard. Hanging from a rawhide string from the wall next to the mirror was a half-toothless comb. I ran it through my matted hair, more to shake the dust loose than to untangle it.

When I stepped outside again, Esteban and the steeldust were gone and Frank Rhodes was standing near his chair. Wordlessly, he came over and handed me two silver dollars.

"What's this?" I asked him.

"Change from your five-dollar gold piece."

"But I thought you said—"

"No charge for filling your waterbags," he said gruffly. "My mistake." And he turned away before I could say anything more and vanished inside the station.

I wondered if he'd changed his mind because I'd told him my wife had passed away. Charity was something I wouldn't take from any man, but this wasn't charity; he'd plainly overcharged me, and whatever the reason, his conscience seemed to have got the better of him. Despite his suspicious nature and his penurious tendencies, I decided Frank Rhodes was a decent man.

Pocketing the silver dollars, I crossed to the eating house. I could smell the aroma of baked beans even before I reached it. Hunger gnawed at my stomach; I hadn't had a proper meal since Jennifer Todd's jackrabbit stew two nights ago. I opened the door and entered.

And came to a standstill one pace inside, staring in surprise, my hand still on the latch. There were two people in there—an elderly, sunbaked woman stirring a kettle on the stove at the far end, and a much younger woman sitting at the puncheon table in the middle of the room, eating from a tin plate.

Well, I'll be damned, I thought.

The young woman was Jennifer Todd.

CHAPTER 7

WHEN SHE REALIZED who I was her eyes widened, then she quickly lowered them to her plate. The fading bruises on her face stood out against her sudden pallor. Her right hand dropped to a carpetbag on the bench beside her; she fingered it nervously.

I shut the door, went to introduce myself to the elderly woman—Frank Rhodes' wife—and then moved over to where Mrs. Todd sat.

"Evening," I said.

When she looked up, her expression was blank, but her eyes betrayed her. She didn't speak.

"You can't have forgotten me that quickly." I sat down across from her. "I haven't forgotten you."

She made an effort to gather herself, but the smile that touched her lips was only a pretense. "I didn't expect to see you again, Mr. Boone," she said, low.

"I reckon you didn't. I didn't expect to see you again, either. Not in such a place as this."

"I . . . changed my mind about leaving my husband."

"Did you?"

"Yes. I'm going to Yuma on the next stage."

"What made you change your mind?"

She started to answer, but Mrs. Rhodes came over with a plate of beans and jerked beef and a cup of coffee, set them down in front of me. There was curiosity in the set of her wrinkled brown face, but she didn't say anything. She returned to the stove and stood watching us while she stirred in the kettle with a wooden spoon.

Jennifer Todd was looking over at where a fire flickered on the room's hearth. Although the fire had been built to ward off the night chill, none of its warmth reached us where we sat. When she realized I was watching her she picked up her fork and began to eat. She chewed as if the food were tasteless, and when she swallowed it was with difficulty.

I said, "I think we should talk, Mrs. Todd."

"About what?"

"About what you took from my saddlebag the other evening."

She stiffened.

"My spare pistol," I said. "Or do you deny that you stole it?"

She hesitated for three or four seconds. Then she let out a breath and said, "I don't deny it, Mr. Boone. I took the pistol, yes—for protection."

"Is that the only reason?"

"Yes. I was already thinking of leaving him then; I knew he'd come after me when he returned and found me gone, that he might find me as he did the other times. I won't go back with him again. That's why I needed the weapon."

"If you were already thinking of leaving him, why didn't you accept my offer of help? I could have given you more protection than that pistol, seen you to Yuma or some other safe place."

"With a man like Mase," she said bitterly, "there are no safe places."

"You didn't answer my question, Mrs. Todd."

"I didn't want to involve you in my trouble. Besides, you were a stranger; I had no knowledge of what kind of man you were. It seemed better for me the other way."

"And now? Would you have me forget it happened?"

"I'd take it as a kindness if you would," she said. "I have a little money; I'll pay you for the pistol. . . ."

"Suppose I ask for its return."

"I . . . I can't return it. I lost it, out in the desert." A beseeching look came into her eyes. "Please, Mr. Boone. Won't you just let me pay you for it? Won't you just accept my apology and let it pass?"

"I could," I said, "but I don't like being lied to."

Her gaze flicked away from me again. "Is that what you think? That I've lied to you?"

"It is. I don't believe you were planning to run away from your husband; I don't believe that's the reason you stole the pistol. I think you took it with the intention of shooting him when he came home."

I tried to keep the accusing note out of my voice, but I was talking about murder, and murder was one thing I could not condone. A flicker of pain, of something that might have been guilt, passed over her face. She pulled her head around to glance over at Mrs. Rhodes, but the other woman was out of earshot at the stove. Jennifer Todd picked up her coffee cup, held it tightly in both hands as if trying to warm them. Her eyes still would not meet mine.

"That's the truth, isn't it, Mrs. Todd?"

It was several seconds before she answered. Then in a resigned way she said, "You yourself said a man like my husband ought to be shot dead."

Hasty words, foolish, coming back to haunt me. "I

did, and I shouldn't have. Was that what put the idea in your head?"

"No. It was nothing I hadn't thought a hundred times before. Look at these bruises, Mr. Boone. I told you this wasn't the first time he beat me; it wouldn't have been the last. Every time it happened, I'd wonder if I would live through it—and then, when it was over, I'd be relieved because I had survived. Until the next time. I lived in constant fear, Mr. Boone. How long would it be before he got drunk and laid hand to me again? How bad would he hurt me? How many more beatings would it take before he finally killed me?"

I picked up my fork, stirred through the beans on my plate without lifting any of the food to my mouth. She had lied to me before, but she was not lying now; the pain in her voice was genuine. I was aware again of the strength in her, a will that would not bend even to a man's cruelty. It was the same kind of strength Emma had possessed, the thing that had made her labor on and on at my side—the thing that had finally cost her her life.

"Do you understand what it's like to live that way, Mr. Boone? Do you have any idea?"

"I think I do," I said. "And I can't say I blame you for wanting him dead, or even for stealing my pistol. But it was mine, Mrs. Todd; that makes me feel partly responsible for his death."

She looked at me again. "Whose death?"

"Your husband's. That's what we're talking about, isn't it?"

"No. I didn't shoot Mase."

"What?"

"I was going to, but the more I thought about it, I knew I couldn't go through with it. I left the ranch before he came home."

I put my fork down slowly, staring at her. "More lies, Mrs. Todd," I said.

"I swear to you, I didn't kill my husband—"

"I rode back to your ranch last night," I said flatly, "after I found the pistol missing from my saddlebag. I found him lying there in the yard with his head half shot away."

"Oh, my God," she said.

"Do you still want to deny it?"

A shudder passed through her. In a half whisper she said, "That wasn't Mase."

"It wasn't—? What are you saying?"

"I shot that man, yes—I admit it. I had no choice. But my husband is still alive."

"Then who was the dead man?"

"I don't know. I never saw him before last night."

"Sweet Jesus. You murdered a stranger?"

"No, it was self-defense. I told you, I had no choice."

"You'd better explain, Mrs. Todd," I said. "And it had best be the truth this time."

"Yes, all right." She looked over at the flames licking up on the hearth; she seemed to find it easier to talk if she didn't meet my eyes. "It happened not long after you left. I was sitting in the cabin with your pistol, trying to find the courage to . . . to do what I felt I had to when Mase came home. But the thought of pointing that pistol at him and just . . . killing him in cold blood was more frightening than all the other fears I'd lived with for so long. After a while I knew I couldn't go through with it. I wasn't lying to you about that."

I said nothing, waiting.

"I decided to hide the pistol," she said, "somewhere Mase couldn't find it. The next time he beat me . . . then maybe I *could* shoot him, because then it would be self-defense. I was looking for a hiding place when the man rode into the yard. I thought it was Mase at first, and I was half frantic because the pistol was still on the table. I took it up and put it inside my sewing basket. Then I heard the man call out, and when I went to the window I saw he was a stranger. I asked him what he wanted. He said he was a friend of Mase's and needed a place to stay, that Mase had told him it was all right to come there. That frightened me all over again. Mase's friends . . . well, I refused to let him in the house."

"And then?"

"He dismounted and came to the door. I tried to put the bar on, but he forced his way inside. He was drunk; he was the same kind of animal as Mase. The way he looked at me . . . you know the way I mean, Mr. Boone."

"Yes," I said, "I know the way you mean."

"He grabbed my arm. When I pulled away from him he shoved me and I fell. I was near the sewing basket; I managed to get the pistol out. I pointed it at him, ordered him to leave. He just laughed and said I wouldn't shoot him. Then he started toward me. I backed out into the yard, warning him, but he lunged at me and tried to take the pistol away, and I . . . I shot him." She shuddered again with the memory. "God, it was awful. His head . . . it exploded. . . ."

"Easy," I said. "What did you do then?"

"I was sick. I sat inside and cried for a time. Then I knew I had to get away from there. If I waited for Mase to come home, and that man really had been a friend of his, he'd have taken it out on me."

"You could have ridden to Maricopa Wells and told the sheriff what happened," I said. "He'd have given you protection."

"Not for more than a day or two. Then Mase would have gotten me alone and beaten me again. I couldn't stand another beating, not after what I'd been through.

I couldn't stand any more killing, either. The only thing I could think to do was to get away as fast as I could. I packed a few things into my carpetbag, took the dead man's horse, and rode into the desert."

"Through the draw at the rear?"

"That way, yes."

"Is that the whole truth, Mrs. Todd?"

"Yes."

"You weren't at the ranch when I rode in?"

"No. I had no idea you'd come back until you told me just now."

"Did you see anyone before or after you left?"

"No one."

"Well, there was somebody at the ranch when I arrived," I said. "Hidden among the pulque cactus out back of the corral. I thought it was you. Whoever it was ambushed me, clubbed me unconscious with a pole."

"It must have been Mase. . . ."

"Maybe. But when I came to, near dawn, I found that my saddlebags had been searched and that the cabin had been ransacked. Literally torn apart. It doesn't make sense your husband would have done that."

"No," she said, soft, "it doesn't."

"It could have been someone who knew the man you shot, knew he'd ridden to your ranch. Do you have any idea why anyone would ransack your home that way?"

"No. I can't imagine."

"Your husband didn't keep anything there of value?"

"Nothing except a few dollars in a Mason jar," she said. "That's all."

"I found two sets of tracks leading through the draw. One of them was yours. It looked as though whoever hit me and ransacked the cabin set out after you."

The fear sparked in her eyes. She didn't speak.

I asked, "Why would this third person have done that? Followed you?"

"I don't know. Unless it was because of . . . what I did to the man who attacked me."

"Mrs. Todd, I started to follow those tracks myself. A group of riders showed up just afterward; they didn't see me, but I watched them from a distance through my spyglass."

"Riders . . . ?"

"A posse, looked like," I said. "One of the men wore a sheriff's star."

She put her cup down in a too-sudden movement that made it clatter on the table. "I . . . don't understand. What would a posse be doing at the ranch?"

"Looking for the man you shot, maybe."

"You mean . . . he might have been an outlaw?"

"It's possible. They could also have been looking for whoever ambushed me and ransacked your cabin." I paused. "Or they could have been looking for your husband."

"Mase?"

"Has he ever been in trouble with the law?"

"He's been arrested for drunkenness more than once, but . . . never anything that would set a posse after him."

"Is he capable of an offense that serious?"

"I suppose he is. Mase is capable of anything."

"Then he could have got mixed up in something in Maricopa Wells. With the man you shot, maybe; with a third man. That might explain it."

"Dear God," she said.

"There's one more thing that happened," I told her. "Last night I stopped at a water tank near the Devil's Highway. Two riders came up as I was leaving; one

of them had been with the posse. As soon as they saw
me, the other man drew his weapon and opened fire.
I was fortunate to get away from them without taking a bullet."

Mrs. Todd shook her head in a bewildered way.
"Why would they shoot at you like that?"

"I don't know. It wasn't because I was seen at your
ranch; I'm positive I wasn't. One of the men was big,
with red hair and a bushy beard. The other one was
small and had long yellow hair. Do you know any
men who answer those descriptions?"

Her hands moved against each other at her breast;
in the lamplight, her eyes were almost black now.
"No," she said. "I hardly know anyone in Maricopa
Wells. Mase seldom let me go into town. As bruised
as I was half the time, he didn't want me going where
people could see what he'd done to me." She pushed
her chair back. "Mr. Boone, I'm sorry you've had so
much trouble; part of it is my fault. But I don't know
the reason for any of it, or what happened in Maricopa Wells. I don't want to know. All I want is to
take the stage tomorrow and travel as far away from
here as I can, far enough so that Mase can never find
me. Will you try to prevent me from doing that?"

"No," I said.

"Then please, can't we both just forget what's been
done to us?"

"I don't know if I can forget it."

She stood, caught up her carpetbag. "I can't bear
to talk about it anymore," she said. "I'll pay you for
your pistol in the morning."

"Mrs. Todd . . ."

But she was already moving away from the table,
and a moment later she was gone.

CHAPTER 8

THE TALK WITH her had robbed me of my appetite. I poked at the food on my plate for half a minute, left it unfinished, and went outside. It was full dark now, almost cold with the night wind up. Mrs. Todd was nowhere in sight; I thought that she had probably gone inside the station. There was no sign of Frank Rhodes or the Mexican hostlers, either.

Across El Camino Real del Diablo, the desert had that ghostly look in the moonlight, silver-white, as if it had been dusted with talcum powder. The yellowish spines of vast clusters of cholla seemed to glow like distant lights. In the distance, toward Mexico, the silhouettes of the Tinajas Altas mountains looked tiny and unreal, like shadows cast up against the sky.

I stood staring out at them, thinking about Jennifer Todd. I wanted to believe what she'd told me; she was badly frightened and vulnerable—a young woman on the run, alone and friendless—and I admired her courage. I felt oddly protective toward her. Maybe it was because I could feel the pain in her, some of the same kind of pain that was inside me. Her life had been hard, and death had come into it, and other trouble, and now she was facing an uncertain future. All of the same was true for me.

But I also felt angry and exasperated, because she *hadn't* told me the truth, or at least not all of it. I was sure of that. She'd answered some questions, but she had created so many others that they were like burrs vexing my mind. She knew one or both of the men who had attacked me. She knew, or suspected, what had taken place in Maricopa Wells that had sent the posse to her ranch. And she hadn't lost my spare pistol; she still had it and she wanted to keep it, for protection in the event her husband found her, or for some other reason.

I wished that our paths hadn't crossed this second time, that I had ridden on and was out there in the desert alone, away from the trouble she'd brought me. I could have forgotten her then, and the rest of it, too. But now the thought that she needed help and that I might be in a position to provide it kept nagging at my mind. Part of it was a matter of wanting to get at the truth, to find out why she'd lied and why I'd been clubbed and almost shot. Part of it was a matter of conscience, just as Frank Rhodes returning those two silver dollars to me earlier had been a matter of conscience; if I took myself out of her life at this point, even though that was what she wanted me to do, Jennifer Todd would plague my thoughts for a long time to come. But the biggest part was that odd protectiveness, that sense of kinship I felt toward her. Whatever she'd done, whatever dark secrets she had locked inside her, she was not a bad woman. I was sure of that, too.

Restlessly, I wandered around the station yard. In the morning, I would try talking to her again; other than that, I couldn't come to a decision as to what to do. It depended on Mrs. Todd and on how things looked to me in the light of a new day.

When the wind began to chill me I went inside the station. Frank Rhodes was alone in the room, sitting at a table in front of the fireplace, a tin cup of coffee before him. The ocotillo branches blazed now on the hearth.

"Supper suit you?" he asked.

"Fine."

"You a drinking man, Mr. Boone?"

"On occasion."

"Got some whiskey, if you're interested."

"I reckon I am."

"Set, then. I'll join you."

"Just let me get my pipe."

He stood and walked behind a short wooden counter. I went to my room, rummaged my corncob and tobacco out of one saddlebag; when I came back, Rhodes had a bottle and a glass at the table. He poured a shot into the glass as I sat down, then added some to his coffee. Under their cottony brows, his eyes studied me while I filled and lighted my pipe.

"Wife tells me you and Mrs. Todd had a long conversation over supper," he said. "Seems you're acquainted with the lady."

"Some. I met her two days ago."

"Mind my asking where that was?"

"Ranch fifty miles east of here. I stopped for some water and she was kind enough to let me have some."

"Her ranch?"

"Yes."

"She have those bruises on her face then?"

"She did. Her husband beat her, she said."

"Told me the same thing. Any man'd do that to a woman is a son-of-a-bitch."

"No argument there, Mr. Rhodes."

"You know this husband of hers?"

I shook my head. "I never met him."

"I'd like to meet him," Rhodes said. "You ever see a mean horse that's been castrated? Ain't so mean anymore."

I took some of my whiskey. It was the first liquor I'd had in weeks, and it burned hot in my throat. "When did Mrs. Todd arrive here?"

"Last evening," he said. "Pretty young woman like that, riding alone on the desert, all beat up—I didn't like to see it. Still don't."

"Neither do I. What did she tell you?"

"Said she'd run off from her husband because he whipped her. Said she was going to California. Seemed scared when I told her the next stage wasn't until tomorrow. Been like that all day; skittish as a newborn colt."

"She's afraid her husband'll come after her."

Rhodes nodded. "He shows up here, he'll regret it. Before or after she's gone on the stage."

"What time does the stage come through?"

"Be here around sunup. Leaves again in an hour."

"Hard travel by day this time of year."

"Hell of a lot worse in the summer," he said. "But it's a mail stage, and the driver and shotgunner are used to it. Passengers ride at their own risk." He studied me over the rim of his cup. "You wouldn't be thinking of taking the stage too, would you?"

"I hadn't thought of it, no."

"Maybe you ought to think of it."

"Why is that?"

"You know Mrs. Todd, you know the trouble she's got. Way you been talking, I figure you're sympathetic. That so?"

"It's so."

"Woman like that oughtn't to be traveling alone. Seeing as how you're just drifting, seems you could see her safe into Yuma, maybe over into California."

"She wouldn't agree to that," I said.

"You ask her?"

"No. But I offered her help two days ago and she wouldn't take it."

"Proud," he said. "Saw that about her first off. But anybody can ride the stage if they're a mind to. Nothing stopping you from signing on anyways, is there?"

"I reckon not. Except for my horse."

"Hitch him up to the coach; been done before. I won't charge you extra for it."

"I don't know," I said. "I'll have to think on it some."

"Wife and I had a daughter," he said then, "only child we were blessed with. Died of diphthcria when she was eight, before we moved out here from Phoenix. She'd be a few years older than Mrs. Todd if she was still alive. About the same age as the wife you lost, I expect."

"About."

His eyes were steady on mine. "You understand what I'm saying, Mr. Boone?"

"Yes, sir," I said, "I do."

"Good. Then you think it over, about taking the stage. Let me know in the morning." He got to his feet. "I'd best see if the wife needs me. Good night to you."

"Good night, Mr. Rhodes."

He went out, and I sat with my pipe and my thoughts for a time. Rhodes' concern for Jennifer Todd added weight to my own. I seemed to be coming to a decision without having to think much on it after all, as if it had been there inside me all along.

At length I went to my room, blew out the lamp before I undressed, and lay down on the bed. Moonlight spilled in through the single window; I draped an arm over my eyes to shut it out.

Jennifer Todd's face appeared in my mind, those

proud eyes with the fear in them and the pain. It stirred something in me, something I didn't want stirred. To drive it away, I allowed the past to come sharp and clear into my thoughts for the first time in weeks—all of it, back to the farm in Ohio where I had grown up.

It was my uncle's farm, not my father's. I had been born in New Mexico, but gold fever had consumed my old man early on and he'd left my mother several times to prospect in California and Arizona Territory. I was five when my mother died in a buckboard accident, and because my father had been away at the time, and nobody knew where, my uncle had come from Ohio and taken me back there. I grew to manhood working his farmland with his sons; but I felt apart from them, an outsider with different thoughts and different dreams. They spent their spare time at games, at making things with their hands. I spent mine with books and visions of the future, of another sort of life somewhere else.

My father came to visit twice during the thirteen years I lived in Ohio. He was the only person I felt close to. I didn't blame him for leaving my mother, for not being there when she died. I understood him and what drove him; I listened to his stories, his adventures, and I knew I was the same kind as he was.

I was eighteen when the war started. I saw in it something both noble and adventuresome—the stuff of the books I'd read, of my father's stories of Indian-fighting and the struggles for freedom in the West. Along with two of my cousins, I joined the Ohio Volunteers and went off to fight with the Union Army.

Four years later, in the fall of 1865, I'd returned a man—but not the same person as the boy I had been. Disillusioned, sickened by the things I'd seen and the things I'd been forced to do. Nights I would wake up with the roar of cannon, the screams of dying men and dying horses echoing in my mind, my body drenched in sweat. I found that I could not stay in Ohio, that there was nothing there for me any longer. I went to New Mexico to visit my father—and found him dying, a shell of the man he had once been.

When the last breath of life went out of him I began to drift, taking work where I could find it in half a dozen states and territories. But I did not travel any farther west than New Mexico; somehow, after having watched my father die, I had no desire to follow the trails he had followed, to see the country that had lured him away from my mother and from me so many times.

For two years I had wandered aimlessly, searching for roots, for an end to the emptiness inside. Searching for myself. And then, one afternoon in a small town in Kansas, Emma had come into my life.

"Oh, I didn't see you standing there. What are you doing here by the milliner's?"

"Waiting for you to come out."

"Whatever for?"

"I saw you walking earlier. I wanted to meet you."

"Well, aren't you the fresh one!"

"I'll apologize if I offended you."

"You didn't offend me. You just . . . surprised me."

"I'm sorry for that, then."

"You're new to Chandlerville, aren't you?"

"I surely am."

"Where do you come from?"

"Nowhere much. I grew up in Chillicothe, Ohio."

"Well, are you planning to stay on here?"

"I might, if the town'll have me."

"Brash young men are always welcome."

"Do you live in town, Miss—?"

"Coulter, Emma Coulter. Yes I do. Why?"

"I'd like to walk you to church on Sunday."

"You don't let a speck of grass grow, do you?"

"Sometimes I don't. Will you agree, Miss Coulter?"

"I don't even know your name. . . ."

"If I tell you, will you agree?"

"I never saw such a one. I don't suppose you'll leave me any peace until I say yes."

"I don't suppose I will."

"Very well, then. I'll let you walk me to church . . . if you tell me your name."

I could still see her as she looked that day. Fine light hair, eyes the color of the sky, tall and slender with tiny hands; just turned eighteen. I had courted her for three months, thought of her every waking minute—and in the evenings, by the light of a lantern in the loft of the stable where I'd found a job, I had begun to write of her. Poetry, sketches . . . the words had flowed from me for the first time, even though I had tried on many an occasion to write, without much success, before the war.

And the more I wrote, the more I saw of her, the more the disillusionment and purposelessness of the previous two years began to fade. I started to live again, to dream again. When she said yes to my proposal of marriage, I knew the first real happiness in my life.

"As soon as we're man and wife, we'll move on. Do you mind, Emma?"

"Not if I can be with you. But why do you want to leave Chandlerville?"

"Not just Chandlerville—Kansas, the plains. This isn't the country for me, for us."

"Where will we go?"

"The Southwest. New Mexico. I was born there, Emma; I can grow there, we both can."

"If it's what you want, Roy."

"It is. It'll be what we both want, you'll see."

And it was, in the beginning. The farm outside Lordsburg, working it together, making it pay; the laughter, the closeness we'd shared, the friends we'd made; the stories and poems written just for her, and the way she'd smiled when I read them to her. But then, in the winter of our third year, Emma had gotten pregnant and then lost the baby in her fifth month, and the doctor had told her she could never have another. Things had begun to change after that. Not between us; our love was as strong as ever, remained as strong to the end. First it was drought, then an insect blight, then a fire that had destroyed the barn and some of the livestock. We had to work long, hard hours to make ends meet. There was less laughter, less joy in our lives. And then—

"I don't feel well, Roy. I don't know what the matter is with me."

"It's just a touch of the ague, that's all."

"I keep having pains in my chest."

"You're working too hard. You have to rest more."

"You can't do all the chores. . . ."

"Yes I can. If you still feel sickly in a day or so, I'll take you in to see the doctor."

"We can't afford the doctor, Roy."

"Never mind about that. You'll see him if you're not better soon."

Two days later she collapsed; two days later she was dead.

The memories were too painful—it was like living it all over again. I swung off the bed, restless, hurting inside, and pulled on my clothing and my boots. I couldn't sleep now; I needed movement, the feel of open space around me.

I left the room and started through the front of the building, past the dying fire. As I neared the door I heard the slow plod of hoofbeats approaching outside. They gave me pause; I was still skittish and wary after what had happened the past two days. Instead of going to the door, I moved over to the window and drew aside an edge of the monk's cloth that curtained it.

A lone rider was approaching from El Camino Real del Diablo. Frank Rhodes was out there, too, coming over toward the station from the eating house, watching the rider move ahead into the yard. I watched him too. At first he was just a dark silhouette; then, as he neared, his features took on definition in the moonlight. I stiffened, felt the muscles cord up across my back.

It was one of the two men who had tried to kill me at the water tank last night—the slight one with the long yellow hair.

I let go of the curtain and hurried back to my room, got my gunbelt, and strapped it on. When I returned to the front window and looked out again, the yellow-haired man had reined in twenty feet from the station door and was sitting his horse with his hands crossed on the saddlehorn. Rhodes stood between him and the building, in close to where his shotgun still leaned against the wall.

The stationmaster said, "Evening," and waited, the way he had with me earlier. Voices carry on the desert at night; I could hear him plainly and hear the yellow-haired man, too, when he spoke.

"Evening. You are stationmaster here?"

"That's right. After lodging for the night, are you?"

"No. I'm lookin' for someone."

"That so? Who?"

"Woman. Ridin' alone."

"Why would a woman be riding alone out here?"

"Ran off from her husband. Her name's Jennifer Todd."

Rhodes spat a stream of tobacco juice into the dust. His voice had an edge to it when he said, "You the husband?"

"Not me. Friend of his."

"Where would he be?"

"Back at his ranch, fifty mile or so."

"How come it's you who's looking?"

"Doin' him a favor, is all," the yellow-haired man said. "You seen a woman alone the past couple of days, old-timer?"

"Nope."

"Sure, now? Her husband's mighty anxious to have her back."

"No woman alone come by here," Rhodes said. He spat again. "Leastwise, none that I seen."

"How about a big fellow, young, ridin' a steeldust horse?"

"Nope. You looking for him too?"

"I am. My friend Todd, he figures this gent had somethin' to do with his wife runnin' off."

"That a fact? I ain't seen nobody riding a steeldust, either. Not many steeldusts in these parts; I'd remember if one come by."

The yellow-haired man studied Rhodes for a time. If the man pushed it, tried to have a look around, I would have to step out and throw down on him. I might have done that anyway, because I had a score to settle with him, if it hadn't been for Jennifer Todd back there at the rear of the building.

But it didn't come to that. The yellow-haired man shrugged at length and said, "Obliged. You see either the woman or the gent on the steeldust, I'll ask you not to mention I was here."

"None of my business," Rhodes said.

"Obliged again." The yellow-haired man started to turn his mount and then paused. "You happen to have a drink of whiskey I can buy? My throat's some parched."

"Water's the best remedy for that."

"Maybe so. But I'm partial to whiskey."

"Sorry, friend," Rhodes said, "we been out of whiskey a week now. Next stage is supposed to bring in a couple of cases."

"Now, don't that figure?" The yellow-haired man grinned sourly. "Keep your powder dry, old-timer," he said, and reined his horse around and rode back toward the Devil's Highway.

Rhodes watched him reach the trail, turn west along it. I watched too, letting out a breath, relaxing my tensed muscles. When the yellow-haired man was out of sight I moved over to the door, opened it, and stepped outside.

The stationmaster turned. I said, "I was inside, listening. I heard it all."

He shifted his cud of tobacco into the other cheek. "Good thing you didn't come out, then. There'd have been shooting, likely."

"I know. I was thinking of Mrs. Todd."

"What that fella said about you helping her to run off from her husband—any truth in that?"

"No, sir. None."

He grunted. "Things you ain't told me, though, Mr. Boone. Like why he's looking for you. Or do you claim he isn't?"

"I guess he is," I said, "but I don't know why."

"Maybe you'd better tell me the whole of it, son."

I saw no reason not to do that. He'd lied to protect Mrs. Todd and to protect me; I owed him that much. "Maybe I'd better," I said.

We went inside, and he poured each of us a shot of whiskey. And I explained everything that had happened over the past two days, everything Mrs. Todd had told me. The only thing I didn't tell him was my suspicion that she had lied about some of it. It was only a suspicion, and there was nothing to be gained in hashing it out with Rhodes.

He said when I was finished, "Whatever happened

in Maricopa Wells, I ain't heard about it yet. But we'll both find out come morning."

"The stage, you mean?"

"Yep. Driver's Jake Sutton; not much goes on that he don't hear about. Anyways, Mrs. Todd's in more trouble than I thought. So are you. I reckon you're both tied up in this together."

"I reckon we are."

"All the more reason for you to stick with her. For all we know, that yellow-haired gent's her husband."

"Same thought crossed my mind."

"You wondering where that redheaded fella got off to?"

"Yes, sir, I am. Could be he's looking for her too."

"Like as not," Rhodes agreed. "You could see to it neither of 'em finds her. You do your thinking on that yet? Make up your mind?"

I nodded. The arrival of the yellow-haired man had done it; but so had the painful memories of Emma, the thought that I had not, in my ignorance, done enough to save her. Maybe I could atone for that by helping to save Jennifer Todd. I owed it to her as a kindness, and to my own peace of mind, to try.

"Mr. Rhodes," I said, "how much is passage on the Yuma stage?"

CHAPTER 9

THE RIM OF the sun was spreading gold above the distant hills when the stage arrived in the morning. I was already up and dressed when I heard the rumble of wheels and the pound of hoofbeats, and I got outside just as the coach rattled to a stop in front of the station.

It was a big steel-and-hickory coach with brass trimmings, painted in a red, gold, and yellow floral design. Its destination—Yuma—was painted on the door panel, and the words *Butterfield Overland Mail* were on the panel under the driver's seat. The driver, a lean, black-haired man with a pock-marked face, swung down; the shotgunner, blond and stocky, followed him. Frank Rhodes was there to greet them. The Mexican hostlers were there too, and they immediately began to unharness the team of four dusty, tired-looking horses.

The driver moved over to open the door so the passengers could step out. There were only three of them: a well-dressed Mexican of indeterminate age, a frail-looking young man in a frock coat who reminded me of a preacher, and a little girl of about seven. The girl's dress was rumpled and her brown hair straggled from her pigtails. She looked around through sleep-bleared eyes, then tugged at the frail man's coat. He took her hand and they followed the Mexican into the eating house.

My future traveling companions, I thought, and briefly wondered about them—who they were and where they were going. Well, their reasons and destinations couldn't be any odder or more vague than mine. That stage would take me to Yuma; after that, I had no idea where I would eventually end up.

The stocky shotgunner also went into the eating house, but the driver tarried to talk to Rhodes. I went over and joined them. Rhodes was saying, "Not many passengers this trip, Jake."

"Nope," the driver agreed. "First time in three months I come through west this empty. Maybe everybody's waiting for the danged railroad to open up so they can travel in style."

"Well, I got a couple of folks'll be joining you here. This here gent's one of 'em. The other's a lady." Rhodes introduced us; the driver's name was Jake Sutton. Then he asked, "Any trouble along the way, Jake?"

"Not so far," Sutton answered. "Spotted a small band of Apache thirty mile the other side of Maricopa Wells, and they trailed us a while at a distance. Made me some uneasy. But nothing come of it."

"Any news from Tucson?"

"None you'd want to hear. Danged railroad's all folks are talking about. Plenty of excitement in Maricopa Wells, though."

"That so?"

"Territorial bank was robbed the other night," Sutton said. "Bandits shot up old Abe Greenbaugh and made off with twenty thousand in greenbacks and gold dust. Poor Abe died the next morning; wasn't nothing the doc could do for him."

Rhodes and I exchanged a glance. He asked, "They get the men who done it?"

"Hadn't when we come through. Posse was still out looking for 'em."

"How many bandits?"

"Three. They all got clean away."

"Any of 'em identified?"

"No. They was wearing dusters and hats, had kerchiefs tied over their faces. Ran down a ten-year-old kid as they was making their escape; busted his arm and two of his ribs. Bastards ought to be hung on the spot when the posse rides 'em down."

"Dutch Bennett don't operate that way," Rhodes said. "He'll bring 'em in to stand trial if he catches 'em."

"Say," Sutton said, "you didn't see three men come past here, did you, Frank? Strikes me they might of headed west for Yuma. West was the direction they rode out of Maricopa Wells."

Rhodes shook his head. "Didn't see three men, no."

"Well, could be they veered off into the desert to hole up or double back east. Dutch'll get 'em, though."

"Or the desert will."

"Now that's a right pleasant thought." Sutton grinned humorlessly. "Reckon I'll get my breakfast now. You want to chin some more, come on in and set with me."

"I'll do that."

Sutton nodded, said to me, "Glad to have you with us, Mr. Boone," and went off toward the eating house.

When the driver was out of earshot, Rhodes said, "You thinking what I am, son?"

"Yeah." I was also thinking that I didn't like the idea at all. The uneasiness was sharp inside me again; I had the feeling I was letting myself in for a lot more trouble than I'd anticipated.

"Man Mrs. Todd shot figures to be one of 'em,"

Rhodes said. "I'd say the other two are the yellow-haired gent and the redhead that was with him when they jumped you, except it don't make sense the redhead would be riding with Dutch Bennett's posse."

"That's not the only thing about this business that doesn't make sense, Mr. Rhodes."

His eyes crinkled, making a fine web of wrinkles. "You figure Mrs. Todd's husband was mixed up in that robbery some way?"

"Seems likely."

"How about Mrs. Todd herself?"

"No," I said, but I wasn't so sure. I wasn't sure of anything just then.

"Me, neither. Man gets so he can judge people, women in particular. She ain't a bad one, Mr. Boone."

"My opinion, too."

"Way things seem, she needs all the help she can get. You ain't changed your mind about taking the stage, have you?"

"No, sir, I haven't changed my mind."

He showed me his store-bought teeth, clapped me on the shoulder. "I didn't reckon you had," he said.

I watched him move off to help the hostlers with a fresh team of horses. My head was full of what Jake Sutton had told us about the bank robbery in Maricopa Wells. And full of questions, too. If the man Mrs. Todd had shot was one of the outlaws, why had he ridden in alone to her ranch? Who were the yellow-haired man and the redhead? Why had they tried to shoot me at the water tank? Why were they, or at least the yellow-haired man, hunting for Mrs. Todd? Was one of them her husband? Or had she lied to me about the man she'd shot, and it really had been Mase Todd I'd found dead at the ranch?

I crossed to the eating house, stepped inside. Jennifer Todd sat at the puncheon table in the same chair she'd occupied last night, wearing a gray serge trav-

eling dress; she was talking to the little girl in pigtails. Mrs. Todd had been in there since before the arrival of the stage; I'd heard her leave her room as I
was dressing. She glanced up at me, nodded slightly,
and resumed her conversation with the little girl.

The impulse I felt was to go to her, tell her I knew
about the robbery in Maricopa Wells, and demand an-
swers to my questions until I got the truth. But it was
neither the time nor the place. There were too many
other people in the room; I would have to get her
alone, and even then there was no way I could force
her to talk to me. She was stubborn and determined
as well as scared, and if I tried to bully her she would
only withdraw into silence. The only way I could see
to get the truth was to befriend her, gain her confidence, pry it out of her piece by piece. And that would
take time and patience—more patience than I felt capable of just now.

Frustrated, I accepted a plate of beans and biscuits
and canned peaches from Rhodes' wife and sat down
next to the preacher, as I'd already come to think of
him, where I could watch Mrs. Todd as I ate. She was
still deep in conversation with the little girl, smiling;
you could tell that she had a fondness for children.
Rhodes had been right in his assessment of her, and
so had I in mine: She wasn't a bad woman. And the
fact that she wasn't made her lies and her secrets all
the more confusing.

The preacher ate in silence, as did the Mexican on
the other side of him; I was glad of that because I
was in no mood for polite talk with strangers. Jake
Sutton and his shotgunner sat apart from the rest of
us, taking their food with good appetite. Rhodes came
in after a time and joined them, and more than once
the three men glanced over at me and at Mrs. Todd.
I wondered what Rhodes was telling the other two.

At length, Sutton tipped his coffee cup a final time

and got to his feet. "Leaving in ten minutes, folks," he announced.

He and Rhodes and the shotgunner trooped out, and I followed them. Rhodes fell into step beside me as I crossed to the station. "I told Jake and Sam about Mrs. Todd being in trouble," he said. "Not the whole of it; that's between you and me. Just that she left her husband on account of he beat her and that you'd volunteered to see her safe out of these parts. Figured they ought to know in case that yellow-haired gent shows up again."

I had no objection to that, and I said so.

"Do me a favor, will you, son?" he asked.

"If I can."

"I'd appreciate knowing how things turn out. When you get to Yuma, or wherever you part ways with Mrs. Todd, write me a letter or send me a collect wire care of Butterfield. Will you do that?"

"Yes, sir, I will."

"Good news don't come my way too often out here," Rhodes said. "I'll be glad to have some."

I went in and got my saddlebags. When I came out, the Mexican and the preacher and his little girl were moving toward the stage, weariness in their steps; they'd no doubt been traveling for some days, numbed by the desert heat and the monotony of the scenery. Mrs. Todd was with them, carrying her carpetbag. The steeldust was tied to the rear of the coach, and when she saw him she stopped, frowning. She transferred the frown to me as I approached.

"You're not taking the stage, Mr. Boone?"

"Yes, ma'am, I am."

"Why?"

"Let's say I prefer to ride in comfort."

"I don't believe that's the reason."

"What other would I have?"

"I don't want you help, Mr. Boone. I told you that."

"I'm not offering it," I said.

She pursed her lips. "I told you all there was to tell last evening. I won't discuss it any further. It's the dead past as far as I'm concerned."

"Have it your way, Mrs. Todd."

Jake Sutton finished loading my saddle into the leather-hooded boot at the rear of the coach and came over to where we were standing. "Put your carpetbag away, ma'am?"

"No, thank you," she said. "I'll keep it with me inside."

He shrugged. I took out a couple of the dime novels I had packed in Lordsburg, to give me something to occupy my time as we rode, and then handed the saddlebags to Sutton for storage in the boot.

The other passengers were already inside. I offered my hand to Mrs. Todd as she lifted her skirts to mount the hanging step plates; she hesitated, then rested her fingers lightly on my wrist and climbed up. When I got inside I saw that the Mexican and the preacher were settled on the leather seat facing forward; the seat in the middle was folded down to make a bed for the little girl. Mrs. Todd had taken the seat that faced to the rear.

The preacher said, "Do you mind if we leave the middle seat as it is? My daughter's very tired."

"Not at all," I said. It gave me a good reason to sit next to Mrs. Todd, and I did that.

She was struggling to raise the canvas curtain on the side window. I leaned over her and grasped the slat, then fastened it with the leather strap. She said, "Thank you," without looking at me.

Jake Sutton cracked his whip, and the coach began to move. I looked out the window on my side. Rhodes still stood there, the morning sun shining in his cotton-colored hair; he raised a hand, and I did the same.

When I glanced back at Mrs. Todd, she was holding something toward me—a folded greenback. "This is the payment I owe you, Mr. Boone. I trust it's sufficient."

I took the greenback, saw that it was a ten-dollar bill, and put it into my shirt pocket. "It's sufficient," I said.

"I hope it settles matters between us."

"Perhaps."

Her mouth turned prim. "We have nothing more to say to each other. I don't mind if you sit next to me, but please don't expect me to make conversation."

"It's a long way to Yuma," I said.

"Just the same, I'll thank you to leave me at my peace."

Beyond her, through the window, the desert shimmered with gathering heat. I wondered what waited out there in the miles ahead. I wondered what waited in here, too, with Mrs. Todd—if she would keep on sitting as tense as she was now, as determined to maintain her silence throughout the next two days.

Yes, it was a long way to Yuma.

CHAPTER 10

THE DAY AND the miles wore on. The coach swung on its leather thoroughbraces in a monotonous rhythm occasionally broken by a sudden, jarring bump that made one or another of us grab for the tug straps. The heat increased steadily as the sun neared its zenith; even with the side curtains lowered, the interior of the coach was stifling. Dust churned up by the wheels filtered inside, clogging the air and making it difficult to breathe.

Mrs. Todd had nothing at all to say to me, although she did make desultory conversation with the preacher, mostly about his little girl. The child herself slept on the middle seat, and the Mexican drowsed on his corner of the seat opposite me. I had not heard him say a word; I judged that he either spoke no English, or spoke broken English and did not want to embarrass himself by saying anything.

I tried reading one of the dime novels—a Beadle pocket novel with what they called an "illuminated" or colored cover, titled *Rattling Dick, the Mountain Outlaw*—but I couldn't seem to concentrate on the words. The heat made it difficult to think, too, and maybe that was for the best. I pulled my hat down over my eyes and drowsed for short periods. Twice, bumps jarred me awake and I caught Mrs. Todd looking at me; but she looked away immediately both times.

Shortly before noon we made a brief rest stop near a grove of saguaro cactus to accommodate the little girl and to water the horses. The desert giants stood, some upward of twenty feet, with their arms twisted skyward; they gave me the fanciful notion, as they always did, that we'd come upon them in the middle of a heated argument they would resume when we went on our way. During the stop, Mrs. Todd spoke again to the preacher—a conversation that ended when he responded to a call from his daughter. That left Mrs. Todd alone in the shade of one of the saguaros, and I took the opportunity to join her.

"You seem to be getting on well with the preacher," I said.

"Preacher? What makes you think that?"

"The way he looks and talks."

"Well, you're wrong."

"It's been known to happen. What is he, then?"

"A schoolteacher. On his way to take a position in Sacramento. His name is Cowdrick."

"Seems I recall a dime novelist named Cowdrick," I said. "But I don't suppose he's the same man."

"I hardly think so. He has been teaching school in El Paso the past several years. His wife's mother took sick, and Mrs. Cowdrick went to California to care for her. She found him his new position, a much better one than in El Paso; he and his daughter are on their way to join her."

"He told you all of that in the short time you've known him?"

"People have always told me things," she said. "I
don't know why."

Well, I knew why. She had a kind face, a sympathetic face; folks responded to that. It was an attrac-
tive face, too—one that the beatings and the hard
desert life had not scarred. Now that the bruises were
fading, I was aware that her sun-dark skin was smooth
and unblemished. A strand of her blond hair had
slipped loose from the tightly wound knot at the nape
of her neck and curled down to brush against her
cheek. That and her fine skin and pretty eyes made
her seem even more vulnerable to me, after the fashion of the schoolteacher's little girl.

The combination of vulnerability and strength was
an unusual one, and yet I had known it before, lived
with it for ten good years: It was the same mixture
Emma had possessed. Mrs. Todd was like Emma in
many ways, it seemed, even though there was no phys-
ical resemblance. In that moment I was conscious of
her as woman, in the same desirous way I had always
been conscious of Emma. The thoughts that stirred at
the back of my mind made me feel as if I were be-
traying Emma somehow.

Yet the stirrings were natural; I could not deny that.
Emma was dead, and I was alive, and a man went on
feeling and needing. Emma had known that, too, perhaps better than I did even now.

Once, when we were sitting before the fire at our
hardscrabble farm, both of us weary from a long day's
work, our talk had drifted to the matter of dying. Now,
thinking back on that evening, it seemed as if she had
suspected that her time was short. She'd said that if
anything happened to her, she hoped I would marry
again. I had laughed at that, told her there was no
chance of anything happening to her, said neither of
us would pass on before our biblical three score and
ten. But she had remained serious, and she'd asked

for my promise that I wouldn't mourn her long, that I'd not spend the rest of my life alone. The odd thing was, I could not remember if I had made that promise, or what I'd said in response.

How well Emma had known me. Known that in spite of my fiddlefoot years, I was not a solitary man. Had I been the one to die young, she would have been able to go on alone, if that was her choice; but I needed someone to share my days and my hopes with, because for the first twenty years of my life I had had no one, and those years of loneliness had left permanent scars. Without a woman, without roots, I would wither inside and become as barren as the gallows land that surrounded me now.

Still, I wasn't sure if I *could* marry again. I could never feel for another woman what I had felt for Emma. She had been my strength and my motivation; she had been perfect for me in every way. How could any other woman take her place? How could I . . . ?

". . . all right, Mr. Boone?"

I blinked, realized that Jennifer Todd was watching me. "Did you say something?"

"I asked if you were all right. You seemed to be in pain. What were you thinking about?"

"My wife," I said.

"Oh? I didn't take you for a married man—"

"I'm a widower," I said. "My wife died four months ago, in Lordsburg."

She said, "Oh," again, in a different voice. Compassion reshaped her expression; her eyes seemed to darken. "I'm sorry, Mr. Boone."

"So am I."

She started to say something else, but the schoolteacher, Cowdrick, appeared with his daughter, and Jake Sutton called out for us to board the coach. I helped Mrs. Todd inside. Sutton's whip cracked as soon as Cowdrick shut the door, and the stage jerked into motion again.

I sat slumped on my corner of the seat with my hat pulled down, letting the stifling midday heat dull my thoughts again. From time to time as the coach rumbled on, I could feel Mrs. Todd's eyes on me, but she didn't speak. No one else spoke, either.

I slept for a while, fitfully, and when I awoke it was late afternoon and the heat was beginning to ease. Cowdrick and his daughter were asleep; so was the Mexican fellow. Jennifer Todd was awake, though, taking a drink from one of the waterbags. When I sat up, mopping at my damp face with my shirt-sleeve, she passed the bag over to me. She watched gravely as I drank.

"Mr. Boone," she said when I was done, "may I ask you a question?"

"You may."

"How did your wife die?"

I hesitated. Then I said, "Her heart gave out."

"But she must have been a young woman . . ."

"She was twenty-eight. We had a farm outside Lordsburg, a poor farm; I don't have to tell you what it's like to live on hardscrabble land. I let her work herself too hard, and it killed her."

"Do you blame yourself?"

"Some, yes."

"Why? Did you know she had a weak heart?"

"No one knew it. But she'd been feeling sickly for days before it happened. If I hadn't let her work herself so hard, she might still be alive."

"That's not for you to say, is it?"

"Meaning?"

"Meaning it might just have been her time."

"The will of God?"

"Yes."

"Maybe so," I said.

"You're not a religious man, Mr. Boone?"

"I used to be. Now . . . I don't know."

It was making me uncomfortable, all this talk of Emma and me and what my beliefs were. I didn't want any more of it because I didn't want any more memories welling up. Mrs. Todd was the one we ought to have been discussing, but I did not quite know how to turn the conversation around without her closing up on me. She seemed friendlier now than she had when we'd left Frank Rhodes' way station; my telling her about Emma had touched something inside her, softened her a little. If I was going to gain her confidence I would have to let her talk about anything she chose and then ask my own questions when the time seemed right.

Still, it was painful to talk of Emma, and I leaned away from Mrs. Todd and lifted the side curtain to peer out. We were climbing into what appeared to be a pass through low hills, and there was nothing to see on that side except a sloping wall of rough-cut limestone. I stretched up and put my head out through the window so I could look downhill along our back trail. El Camino Real del Diablo was empty as far as I could see. Traveling through the heat of day, we hadn't come on anyone else headed west, or east—no one I'd been aware of, anyhow.

I pulled back inside. The leather seat was stuffed with horsehair and it was soft enough, but all the days I'd spent in the saddle had stiffened the muscles in my back and hips; no matter how I sat, I felt discomfort. I shifted on the seat until I had my back wedged up against the side wall and one boot anchored on the edge of the folded-down middle seat where the schoolteacher's little girl was sleeping. That position, at least, eased the pressure on my tailbone.

Mrs. Todd had taken a couple of crochet hooks and some yarn out of her carpetbag; the hooks made little clicking noises as she worked them together. They were the only sounds inside the coach for a time, except for the Mexican's breathy snoring.

But it wasn't long before she said, "Do you have any children, Mr. Boone?"

"No. No children."

"Didn't you want any?"

"We did. But my wife miscarried once some years back, and the doctor told us it wasn't possible for her to try again."

"I'm sorry about that, too," she said.

I nodded. "And you? Did you want children?"

"Very much, at first. But Mase . . . he didn't, and even if he had, I wouldn't have suffered a poor infant with a father such as him."

"You're young yet," I said. "There'll be another man someday. And children."

"Not for a long time. Perhaps not ever."

"All men aren't like Mase Todd."

"Of course not. I'm not sour on the sex, Mr. Boone. But I intend to be very careful about trusting any man again."

"So I've noticed," I said.

She didn't say anything. The crochet hooks kept on clicking, rhythmically, and her eyes were steady on them. I thought she was finished talking, that I'd done what I had been worried about doing—closed her off. I started to pull my hat over my face again.

Mrs. Todd said, "Will you tell me her name?"

"Whose name?"

"Your wife's."

"Emma," I said. "Her name was Emma."

"That's a pretty name."

"She was a pretty woman. A beautiful woman."

"The way you say that . . . you must have loved her very much."

"Yes," I said, quiet. "Very much."

"May I ask how you met her?"

I explained briefly how it had come about; how I had been drifting since the end of the war.

"What was it like, fighting in the war?" she asked.

"Ugly. Very ugly."

"Is that all you have to say about it?"

I thought again of the long marches, the cold nights huddled around the campfires, the roar of the cannon and the clash of sabers, the sightless eyes and torn flesh of friends and of strangers. "That's all," I said. "I don't like to talk about it, or remember it."

She nodded and let it go. Emma had been that way too, recognizing that there were some things too painful to talk about. She'd realized I was not withholding anything from her, and she had never let it create a distance between us.

Mrs. Todd was through speaking this time. And so was I; the memories, the ghosts were crowding my mind again. The remainder of the afternoon passed in silence.

At dusk we came on the next way station. The 'dobe buildings and surrounding terrain were so much the same as the one run by Frank Rhodes that I had the fancy we'd gone around in a circle instead of ahead in a straight line.

Wordlessly the five of us climbed out of the coach. The others trooped toward the eating house, but I moved over to where the stationmaster—a fat, balding man with heavy jowls—was directing his hostlers as they unharnessed the weary team of horses. Jake Sutton was standing with him.

I asked the stationmaster if a yellow-haired man had been by looking for Jennifer Todd. He wanted to know why it was my business. Sutton explained the situation for me; or as much of it as Frank Rhodes had let him in on.

The stationmaster, whose name was Turnbull, said, "Fella looked like that did stop by today, midmorning. Told him I hadn't seen the woman he was hunting for. He bought himself some breakfast and rode on, headed west."

"Was he alone?" I asked.

"Yep."

"Have you seen a big redheaded man with a bushy beard in the past two days? Riding a roan horse?"

Turnbull shook his head. "Yellow-haired gent's the only lone rider I seen in most a week."

I thanked him and left him and Sutton to their own conversation. The yellow-haired man, it seemed, was determined to ride all the way to Yuma on his search for Mrs. Todd; and he was in a hurry about it, too, pushing his horse, riding with only short rest stops, to have reached this station by midmorning. I would have to be watchful for him in Yuma. Chances were, he would make it there a half day ahead of us and still be in town when we arrived.

As for the redhead, I still had no idea what had happened to him. Had he gone off hunting for Mrs. Todd in the other direction, back toward Maricopa Wells? Or had the yellow-haired man had some sort of trouble with him, left him dead or dying out on the desert?

Supper here was the same as it had been at Rhodes' station: beans and jerked beef, with a pie made from canned peaches for dessert. A silent Mexican woman did the cooking and serving. Mrs. Todd and the others were already finished up when I came inside; she didn't have anything to say to me, and while I was getting my portion she went off somewhere with Cowdrick's little girl. I ate without any wasted time, because I was hungry; but it didn't seem to taste. Neither did the pipe that I packed and lit when I was done.

I walked outside and looked at the purple-black sky

stretching vast above me, the silver stars all aglitter and the fat hanging moon. Nights like this, you could almost believe there was something to this world that made sense, some order, some purpose. But then, it had been a night like this that Emma died. . . .

Fifteen minutes later, we were all back aboard the coach. And two minutes after that, the Butterfield Overland Mail was on its way again, less than twenty-four hours out of Yuma.

CHAPTER 11

IT WAS COOL in the coach now that night had fallen, and that made it easier to breathe and to rest. After the first few minutes, there was no conversation. The night wind came up and blew chill through the side curtains, so that Cowdrick and I had to tie them down. Mrs. Todd wrapped herself in a paletot and a shawl and burrowed into the far corner of the seat. I put on my coat and did the same on my side. The swaying of the coach, the heavy darkness let me sleep right away—much more deeply than I had during the day.

I was awake at dawn, stiff and sore. Mrs. Todd and the other three passengers slept until we pulled into the last of the way stations a half hour later. While the others trooped in for breakfast I spoke briefly to Jake Sutton. Both he and his shotgunner looked rested; they were used to this kind of travel and would have managed to take turns sleeping up on the box. Then I questioned the stationmaster about the yellow-haired man. That one had stopped here, too, late last night, again asking about Mrs. Todd. There was little doubt that he would be in Yuma by the time we arrived.

We were back on the road within an hour. I took up the Beadle pocket novel again and tried to read, but the story was poor—full of conniving scouts, bloodthirsty Indians, and misinformation about life in the West, and featuring a hero who got himself out of predicament after predicament much too handily. I could not maintain any interest in it, and after a time I put it down.

Mrs. Todd said, "You don't seem to be enjoying your book."

I glanced over at her. She had been disinclined to talk earlier, at the way station, but judging from her expression, the boredom had begun to take its toll; she seemed willing now to be drawn into conversation.

"It's not very good," I said.

"Dime novels generally aren't."

"Have you read any of them?"

"Yes, when I was younger. Not since I married Mase. They're all the same."

"They don't have to be," I said. "I could write better ones than most myself."

"Could you? How would you write them better?"

"More realistically. No one ever massacred an entire Indian tribe before breakfast."

She smiled faintly. "The heroes never seem to have real feelings, do they? Or lives like the rest of us—families, problems, dreams?"

"No, they don't."

"Do you fancy yourself a writer, Mr. Boone?"

"I've written a few things. Short stories, poems, sketches." Now, why had I told her that? My dreams of being a writer were private, something I had shared with no one but Emma.

"Really?" Mrs. Todd said. "Were they published?"

"No. I never tried to have them published."

"Why not?"

"I don't know. I suppose . . . well, I suppose in a way I was embarrassed."

"For heaven's sake, why?"

"Writing shows the sensitive side of a man," I said. "Out here, some folks equate sensitive with weak."

"Nonsense. It's a special kind of man who has a sensitive side to his nature."

"Maybe so."

"If you'll excuse me," Cowdrick said from the other seat, "I couldn't help but overhear. Mrs. Todd is quite right, you know. What the West needs is more sensitive, articulate people—writers, teachers, political leaders. It is they, not the uneducated commoner, who will shape the future of this part of the country."

"Pretty speech, Mr. Cowdrick. But to my way of thinking, the man who works with his hands is just as important in the scheme of things as the man who works with his mind. More so, maybe."

"If he is educated and shown the proper course—"

"No, sir. Educated or not, intelligent or not, directed or not. It's honest, hardworking men and women the West needs most. Given enough folks like that, the future will take care of itself."

Cowdrick pursed his lips. He didn't agree with my outlook, and under different circumstances he might have gone on to give me an argument; as it was, with the heat starting to rise again and dust thickening the air, he fell silent. And minded his own thoughts from then on.

After a time Mrs. Todd said, "You're a curious man, Mr. Boone. You worked a hardscrabble farm for ten years, and yet you also wrote poems and stories. Which is it you really want to be, a farmer or a writer?"

"My being a writer is just fancy, that's all."

"Is it? Well, why don't you try to have something published just the same? Why don't you write a dime novel if you think you can?"

"I might, when I get where I'm going."

"And where is that?"

"I don't know yet."

"You haven't any destination in mind?"

"No. I'm just drifting now, but I'll know when I get to a place I want to settle in."

"I wouldn't care for the uncertainty of that," she said. "I know just where I intend to settle."

"Where would that be, Mrs. Todd?"

She didn't answer. Instead she leaned over and lifted the side curtain to peer out at the barren terrain. At the end of several seconds she said, "I hate this desert. I've hated it since the first day I came here."

"When was that?"

"Three years ago."

"Where are you from originally?"

She let go of the curtain and faced me again. "Oklahoma," she said. "Eastern Oklahoma, in the foothills."

"I was there once, long ago. It's pretty country."

"Very. Small lakes, limestone cliffs, sycamore trees. I loved the sycamores, the way they would change with the seasons. There aren't any trees like that out here; everything is always the same—hot and desolate and ugly."

"Some people who've lived here all their lives would disagree."

"I suppose so. Oh, there are some things I liked, I admit that. The early mornings, when the cactus flowers bloomed. But cactus flowers only last a short time."

I'd seen those flowers myself. Some opened once, then closed and never bloomed again. Such short lives, too short—like the bloom of Emma's life before work and hardship had robbed her of it . . .

But I did not want to start thinking that way again. I said, "Is it back to Oklahoma that you intend to go?"

She hesitated. "No," she said, "there is nothing there for me any longer."

"No family?"

"Plenty of family. That's the problem; my people are dirt poor. I would only be another mouth to feed. Besides, they would never let me forget my marriage was a failure."

"Why wouldn't they? You married young; young people make mistakes. They're entitled to them."

"Not in my family's eyes. I ran off with Mase, married him against my father's wishes. I was eighteen at the time; he couldn't stop me, but he believed I was old enough to know better." Her mouth quirked bitterly. "As it turned out, he was right."

"Fathers usually are about things like that."

"I didn't think so at the time. I'm the oldest of six children; after my mother died when I was eleven, I helped raise my brothers and sisters."

"And you grew tired of that chore?"

"No, it wasn't like that. My father remarried just before my eighteenth birthday. Two women trying to run the same household—it makes for problems. I felt it was time I had a house of my own."

"I see."

"You're wondering what I saw in a man like Mase, aren't you? I mean, I've told you I like sensitivity in a man, and he has none of that."

"The thought has crossed my mind more than once."

"I was young and naïve when I met him," she said. "He came through our town on his way back to Arizona; he'd come East to work for a year with his brother in St. Louis. He had money from that, and plans to buy a ranch out here, and he turned my head with his talk of what he hoped to accomplish. At the time he seemed quite a man to me. Strong, able to handle the world on his terms. It was only later I found out that everything had to be on his terms.

"Arizona was a disappointment, and so was that

ranch he bought, and so was Mase. Still, I tried to make the best of it: I thought things would get better. But they only grew worse and worse. He didn't want a wife—he wanted a slave. Someone to cook, sew, and keep his house while he went off and did as he pleased. And of course when he was drunk or badly hung over, what he wanted was someone to bully."

"That part of your life is over now," I said. "You won't make that same mistake again."

"No, I surely won't."

"Where *will* you go, if not back to Oklahoma?"

"Does it really matter, Mr. Boone?"

"I'm just curious."

Again she hesitated. But then she shrugged and said, "To San Francisco, if you must know. I've always dreamed of going there—a place where it's cool and there is water all around and fine homes and well-bred people."

"What will you do there?"

"At first I thought I might open a small dress shop; I'm good with my needle. But then I thought no, what I enjoy most is taking care of others. Cooking, making do for them. Helping to raise my brothers and sisters taught me that, I suppose. So I'm going to rent a house, a big one with several rooms, and open it to paying guests."

"A boardinghouse?"

"Yes. But not just an ordinary boardinghouse. A home for people who have no home of their own. I can be independent that way without ever having to be alone. I was alone so much those years with Mase."

"How will you pay for it?" I asked. "It must be expensive to rent a house in San Francisco."

"Well, I couldn't do it immediately, of course. I'll take a job first and save every penny I can until I have enough."

"Do you intend to travel straight to San Francisco from Yuma?"

"On the first downriver steamer."

"Passage all that way is costly," I said. "Have you enough money to buy it?"

"Yes." She glanced over at Cowdrick; his eyes were closed and he appeared to be dozing. But she lowered her voice just the same. "I . . . well, Mase kept some greenbacks in a Mason jar hidden in the corral; he used it for gambling. He didn't think I knew about it, but I did."

"So you took it."

"It's my money too, Mr. Boone."

"I reckon that's so."

"I worked harder for it than he did," she said.

"He won't be looking at it that way."

"I don't care what he thinks, not anymore."

"The point is, Mrs. Todd," I said, "from what you've told me about him he considers you and that money his property. That makes him relentless enough to follow you all the way to San Francisco."

"No," she said, "he can't do that."

"Why can't he?"

"He doesn't have money for passage. Every dollar he had was in that Mason jar."

"You could be wrong about that, you know. He might have plenty of money now."

"What do you mean? How could he have plenty of money?"

"He could," I said, "if he was involved in that robbery in Maricopa Wells."

She jerked as if I'd struck her. Her eyes widened and I saw the fear in them again. "Robbery? What robbery?"

"The bank was held up the same day you ran off. By three men, masked, wearing dusters. You didn't know about that?"

"No. How would I know?"

"That was what the posse was doing at your ranch the following morning—looking for the bandits. It could be they went there because they felt your husband was one of the three men."

She opened her mouth to speak, but no words came out. She shook her head.

"The man who attacked you might have been one of them too. So might the yellow-haired fellow and the redhead with the bushy beard who tried to kill me." I paused. "One of those two is your husband, isn't he?"

"No," she said. She moved farther away from me on the seat, hard against the side wall.

"Mrs. Todd, listen to me . . ."

"Leave me alone, Mr. Boone. Leave me alone!"

She said it loud enough to wake up Cowdrick and the Mexican. They peered over at us in a startled way. "Is something the matter?" Cowdrick asked.

I said, "Nothing's the matter."

"Mrs. Todd?"

"Would you mind changing places with me?" she asked him. "I'd prefer to sit over there."

"Is this man bothering you?"

"With words, yes. I'd rather not sit next to him any longer."

Cowdrick glared at me as he and Mrs. Todd traded places. He kept on glaring from time to time, but he didn't speak. Mrs. Todd picked up her crocheting again, sitting stiffly, her lips a thin white slash.

I had handled things badly, pressing her as I had. It had seemed to be the time for plain talk, but all I had succeeded in doing was shattering the intimacy that had begun to develop between us.

I opened the side curtain and stared out. The terrain was less arid here, beginning to give way to more fertile, cultivated land as we drew closer to Yuma. In the distance, paralleling El Camino del Diablo, I could see the gleaming steel of the partially completed Southern Pacific rail line.

Damn, I thought. Damn!

Now how was I going to get the truth out of her?

CHAPTER 12

IT WAS EARLY evening when we finally arrived in Yuma.

My father had described it to me as a collection of adobe buildings and Mexican *jacales* sprouting in three different locations above and below Yuma Crossing; but it had been before the war that he'd come through it the last time. Now, twenty years later, it was a settled community with streets and more frame houses than 'dobes, extending south from Fort Yuma. The plank sidewalks were crowded with soldiers, railroad workers, townspeople, Mexican and Indian laborers, ranchers and farmers and travelers bound east across the desert or west to California or north via steamer to the mining towns along the Colorado.

When the coach clattered to a stop at the depot I tried to help Jennifer Todd alight; she shrugged off my hand. She hadn't spoken to me since the incident that morning, and she said nothing at all to me now. She went to where Jake Sutton was opening the rear boot and asked him the location of the nearest hotel.

"That'd be Yuma House. Next block over on First."

"Is it a good hotel?"

"Best there is in town, ma'am."

"Thank you."

She moved away from Sutton and from me, but she didn't set out for Yuma House just yet; she paused to say good-bye to Cowdrick and his daughter. That gave me time to get my saddlebags out of the boot and to ask Sutton to hold the steeldust here for a few minutes. He said he would. He expected to remain at the depot at least half an hour.

Mrs. Todd was still talking to Cowdrick's little girl, so I packed my pipe as I waited nearby. It was cooler with night coming on and a light breeze stirring the air, and I felt the need of a smoke; I had not had one all day, in deference to the heat and to the other passengers. I scanned the faces of men lounging in the vicinity and of the passersby, but none of them belonged to the yellow-haired man or to his redheaded partner.

From where I stood, I could see the fort, big and imposing on its hill, fronted by squares of surprisingly green lawn. Some distance away, atop another hill, was Yuma Territory Prison—opened just four years and already notorious in the Southwest, dubbed by its inmates the "Hell Hole." In the fading sunlight, it looked stark and grim against the backdrop of the distant mountains, like a photograph of a medieval fortress I had once seen in a book.

But it was what lay below to the west that interested me most. Yuma Crossing—the confluence of the Gila and Colorado rivers, gleaming in the last light of day. Steamers waiting at the wharves, a long row of warehouses, freighters laden with cargo from San Diego and San Francisco, even a shipyard over on the Colorado side. And the reddish, silt-heavy waters of the Colorado, moving swiftly on their way to the sea. A hungry river, my father had called it, without mercy in its heart; but to me, seeing it for the first time, it held a primitive beauty that filled me with a sudden sadness. It was a sight Emma would never see, a river she would never cross or travel upon. I had a feeling that when I crossed it myself, a part of my life—the part Emma belonged to—would be over too, and I would be a different man from then on. I could never go back to Lordsburg once that step was taken; I could never return to what once had been.

It anguished me some, thinking that way. But mixed with the anguish and the sadness was a stirring of old emotions I had locked away inside for ten years: a wanderlust, a yearning for new places and new experiences. Maybe there was a positive future for me after all, somewhere over there in the haze-streaked vastness of California. Maybe I *would* find new roots, a new sense of peace . . .

Mrs. Todd finished her good-byes and started away along the boardwalk. She hadn't taken more than a dozen strides before I fell into step beside her. "I'll carry your carpetbag for you if you like," I said.

She stopped abruptly and faced me; her eyes were angry. "I suppose you're going to Yuma House too?"

"I am."

"Why?"

"Because I need a place to stay, same as you. And because you need someone to look after you."

"I don't need any such thing . . ."

"Yes, you do. The yellow-haired man I told you about rode into Frank Rhodes' way station the night before we left, asking for you. He said he was a friend of your husband's and was looking to bring you back. Mr. Rhodes allowed as how he hadn't seen you, and the fellow rode on. He stopped at the other two stations, too, which probably means he's come right on into Yuma. He might even have taken a room at Yuma

House. You wouldn't care to walk in alone and find him sitting there waiting, would you?"

Her face had gone pale. "No," she said, low. "I wouldn't."

"So you see? You do need looking after, whether you like the idea or not. I don't believe you ought to go on to San Francisco alone, either. In fact, I'm thinking I might take a packet there myself—also whether you like the idea or not."

She didn't say anything. But she no longer looked angry; just frightened.

"Mrs. Todd," I said, "who is the yellow-haired man?"

"I don't know."

"How about the red-haired one with the beard? You don't know who *he* is either, I suppose?"

"No." She bit her lip. "Do you think he's here in Yuma too?"

"Maybe." I let a couple of seconds pass. "I'm going to find out the truth sooner or later, you know," I said then. "You'll save us both time and trouble if you confide in me."

"I've already told you the truth—"

"Not all of it. Why is the yellow-haired man after you? The real reason."

"I don't know."

"It has something to do with the bank robbery in Maricopa Wells, doesn't it?"

"I don't *know!*"

"All right. We'll leave it at that for now. But only for now."

I set off again. She stood her ground, but only for a moment; then she was at my side, staring straight ahead. She was more afraid of the other two than she was of me.

Yuma House was a large, whitewashed structure that looked more like a small fort than a hotel. Three men were sitting on the front porch, but all of them were elderly and all of them were strangers to me. Inside, the lobby was deserted except for a fat man in a too-tight frock coat seated on a high stool behind the desk. He had rooms available, but before we registered I described both the yellow-haired man and the redhead, saying that they were friends of mine, and asked if either one had taken a room there. The clerk shook his head; he hadn't seen anyone who looked like them, he said.

When we had our keys, Mrs. Todd requested that a bath be drawn for her. Then we went past the entrance to the hotel dining room and upstairs to the second floor, and I walked with her to her room.

"I have to return to the depot and attend to my horse," I said. "I should be back within the hour."

"Are you sure you wouldn't rather stand guard over me while I bathe, Mr. Boone?"

It was a foolish question and I didn't answer it. Instead I said, "I expect we'll both be hungry by the time I get back. If you have no objections to eating with me, we can take supper together."

"Perhaps I prefer to eat alone."

I shrugged. "In that case, we'll sit at separate tables. Or would you also prefer we eat at different times?"

"Oh, all right," she said in a resigned way. "I'll take supper with you. But I won't answer any more of your questions."

"I'll call for you in an hour or so."

My own room was at the other end of the hall. It was small but clean, with a comfortable-looking four-poster bed; the windows faced toward the river. I put my saddlebags on the bed and then left the room and the hotel and walked back up to the stage depot.

Jake Sutton was inside, and he took me out to the

corral to where the steeldust had been picketed. "Everything all right at the hotel?" he asked.

"Yes."

"Well, I hope Mrs. Todd doesn't have any trouble here. Fact there wasn't none on the road is a good sign, I reckon."

"I'll see to it that she doesn't," I said. "Can you tell me where the nearest livery stable is?"

"Two blocks west. Owner's name is McGee."

"Is he a fair horse trader?"

"He won't cheat an honest man," Sutton said. "You going to sell your steeldust?"

"If I can get a decent price. I'm thinking of taking a steamer to San Francisco. Do you know when the next downriver boat leaves?"

"Tomorrow morning. Boats don't travel the Colorado at night—too many snags and channels. Couldn't get the Cocopahs to work on the river after dark anyway."

I nodded. Most of the deckhands on the Colorado riverboats were Cocopahs, Yuma Indians, and one of their superstitions was that the river spawned demons that prowled in its mists after dark; when the boats tied up at night, the Cocopahs left them and did their sleeping on shore.

"Place you want to go," Sutton said, "is the Colorado Steam Navigation Company offices. Next block down from Yuma House."

"Would they still be open?"

"Until after ten on nights before sailing."

I thanked him and we shook hands, and I untied the steeldust and went looking for the livery stable. It turned out to be a big adobe building with one of its doors standing open and lamplight glowing inside. I led the horse through the doorway. The owner, McGee, a stocky, brown-haired man in patched overalls, came out of one of the stalls to greet me. I told him Jake

Sutton had sent me over and that I was interested in selling the steeldust.

"That so? How much you asking?"

"I'll make a fair offer."

McGee liked to haggle, but the price we settled on was satisfactory. While he went to get the money I rubbed the steeldust's muzzle by way of saying good-bye. He was a good horse and I'd miss him. But selling him was just one more in a series of things ending. That was what I'd come West for, wasn't it? Endings and beginnings?

When I got back to my room at Yuma House I stripped off my dusty clothes, washed up, shaved, and put on my last clean shirt and Levi's. Then I went down the hallway and knocked on Mrs. Todd's door.

She was wearing the same gray serge traveling dress, but she had beaten the dust out of it and smoothed out the wrinkles. With her blond hair piled on top of her head, she looked fresh and young and pretty; her fading bruises were all but invisible under an application of powder and rouge. She also seemed less antagonistic toward me than she had been earlier. The smile she gave me was small but it appeared genuine.

A little awkwardly, I said, "You look very nice, Mrs. Todd."

"Thank you. A bath does wonders for a person. I'd almost forgotten how good a bath can be, it has been so long since I had one. There never seemed to be enough water at the ranch."

"I wouldn't mind a bath myself. But I didn't want to take the time before supper."

"You did shave and change clothes, though. Was that for my benefit?"

"I thought it proper."

"You're a very proper man, aren't you, Mr. Boone?"

"I try to be. Shall we go down to the dining room?"

We took a table at the rear of the large, plain room. The fare was plain, too—beefsteak, vegetables, eggs, and a half-dozen simple Mexican dishes. We both ordered beefsteak, corn, and coffee.

"Not much to choose from, was there?" I said when the waitress had gone. "Nothing like the hotels in San Francisco."

"How do you know? I thought you'd never been to San Francisco."

"I haven't. But I knew a fellow who lived there for a couple of years. He told me about the dining room in a hotel called the Occidental—crystal chandeliers, sterling silver, French waiters, and a fantastic variety of food."

"Really?"

"Yes. Oysters and champagne to start, then fish, duck, roast beef—each one served with a different wine—and French pastries and brandy for dessert. And all the trimmings too, of course."

"My," she said, impressed. "Your friend must have done well to afford such fancy meals."

I smiled. "So he claimed, but I have my doubts. I don't believe he ever ate meals like that; I believe he *served* them. My suspicion is that he was one of the 'French' waiters he told me about."

Mrs. Todd laughed. She had a fine laugh, rich and robust. Like Emma's, I thought—yet another thing about her that reminded me of Emma.

"I don't suppose I'll ever eat such a meal, either," she said. "At least, not for a long time to come."

"Perhaps you'll make good sooner than you think."

"Perhaps. But . . . well, I've been thinking and I've decided not to go directly to San Francisco after all."

"Oh? Why is that?"

"I don't have all that much money, and the prospect of trying to find a respectable job in such a large city concerns me. I would be better off if I went somewhere else first, to a place I know I can get work; that way I can save enough money to go to San Francisco later on without having to worry."

"Where would that place be?"

"Callville. I have a cousin there."

"That's in Nevada, isn't it?"

"Yes. The last town on the Colorado that is serviced by the steamers. My cousin owns a general store in Callville; he'll give me a job and he'll let me stay in his house."

"So you'll be taking an upriver steamer instead of a downriver boat?"

"Yes."

"Does your husband know about this cousin of yours?"

"Are you thinking Mase might follow me there?"

"It's a possibility, isn't it?"

"Not really," she said. "I may have spoken of my cousin a time or two, but Mase never paid any attention to anything I said. He had no interest at all in my family."

"Just the same, I'd feel better knowing you arrived safely in Callville."

She sighed. "I suppose that means you'll be booking upriver passage too?"

"It's for your own good, Mrs. Todd."

"Yes, I guess I've come to accept that." She sighed again. "If we're going to continue to be traveling companions, you may as well call me by my given name. I hate 'Mrs. Todd'; I'm not going to be Mase Todd's wife much longer. Or does calling me Jennifer offend your sense of what is proper?"

"No," I said. "I'll be pleased to call you Jennifer"— the name tasted odd on my tongue, curiously intimate—"if that's what you prefer."

"I do. And may I call you Roy?"

"Of course."

"Good. That's settled, then."

Our food came, and we ate mostly in silence. The beefsteak was passably good, the corn tolerable, and the coffee as bad as any I had ever brewed for my- self. The waitress suggested apple cobbler for dessert, but neither Jennifer nor I was willing to gamble on it; the peach pies we'd had at the Butterfield way sta- tions had destroyed both our appetites for sweets.

Out in the lobby, I said to her, "The steamship of- fice is still open; I might as well go down and buy passage for us tonight."

"I'll go with you—"

"No. I think it would be best if you didn't show yourself on the street. I'll pay for both tickets and you can reimburse me when I return."

I waited until she went upstairs, and then I left the hotel. The boardwalks were still crowded; if anything, more people had been drawn out by the evening cool. From one of the windows above a feed store, a gui- tar sounded the mournful notes of a Mexican love song; inside a saloon I passed, someone was playing "Buffalo Gal" on an out-of-tune piano. The music and the milling people gave the night a festive quality.

There was no sign of the yellow-haired man or his red-headed friend, either on the sidewalks or at the Colorado Steam Navigation Company office. With part of the money I had removed from my boot at Yuma House earlier, I paid for two cabin passages to Call- ville, a long 660 miles upriver. The clerk told me that the steamer *Mohave,* "the pride of the line," was sched- uled to depart at eight o'clock in the morning.

I saw no one I recognized on the walk back to the hotel. When I knocked on Jennifer's door she let me wait a minute or two before she opened it. Her mood seemed to have changed again since dinner; she was solemn and fretful, as if there were things weighing heavily on her mind.

"Were you able to buy passage?" she asked.

"Yes. A cabin for each of us."

"How much was my fare?"

I told her, and she took a small sheaf of green-backs from the pocket of her dress and counted out the full amount. She did not have much left when she was done.

"May I have my ticket?"

I gave it to her. "The steamer leaves at eight o'clock," I said. "I'll call for you at seven; that should allow · us plenty of time."

"All right." She hesitated, then surprised me by extending her hand. Her fingers were cool and soft; the feel of them made me aware again, uncomfortably, of how desirable she was. "I know I haven't been very pleasant to you," she said, "but I do appreciate all you've done. I mean that sincerely."

There was nothing I could think of to say to that. I said only, "I'll see you in the morning, then. Good night, Jennifer."

"Yes," she said. "Good night, Roy."

She closed the door and I heard the bolt slide into place. In my room, I undressed and got into bed. But sleep would not come right away. She was still on my mind—the same constant struggle between thoughts of her and thoughts of Emma. I was becoming too attached to Jennifer Todd, this woman I barely knew, this woman who had stolen my gun and killed a man and lied to me. It would be a relief, I told myself, when we reached Callville and she was no longer a part of my life.

But I could not quite make myself believe it. It wouldn't be easy to say good-bye to her in Nevada. What worried me was that I would not *want* to say good-bye when the time came. . . .

CHAPTER 13

IT WAS A hot, sweaty sleep that I awoke from at first light, and I did not feel particularly rested. As I stretched and then swung my feet to the floor, I wondered what it would be like to pass a night in comfort and ease, free of worry and grief. It had been so long since I'd had a restful night, I had difficulty recalling how it felt.

I stood at the window for a moment, looking out past the chintz curtains. The sky was steel gray, and shadows still clung to the buildings of Yuma spread out below. Thin mists coiled above the waters of the Colorado, drifting upward like smoke and then fading into nothingness. At the wharf where the steamers were tied, there already seemed to be a good deal of activity.

Lighting the lamp, I carried it to the washbasin and splashed my face and body with cold water. Then I dressed, strapped on my gunbelt, and gathered up my saddlebags. If Jennifer was up and ready to leave, I judged there was still time for a cup of coffee in the hotel dining room. I went out, walked down the hall to her room, and knocked on the door.

There was no answer. I knocked again; still no response. On impulse I tried the knob, found it unlocked, and opened the door and glanced inside. The room was empty. Both Jennifer and her carpetbag were gone.

I hurried downstairs and looked into the dining room, thinking that perhaps she'd come down early for coffee and something to eat. But the three people seated at tables there were all men. A feeling of concern stirred inside me. Frowning, I crossed to the desk.

A different clerk—thin, pale, balding—was on duty. I described Jennifer and asked him if he had seen her this morning.

"Why, yes, sir, I have," he said. "She turned in her key a half hour ago."

"Did she say why she was leaving so early?"

"No, she didn't."

Damn, I thought, what was this about? It could be she had grown restless and instead of waiting for me, had left for Yuma Landing by herself. Which was foolish enough because the yellow-haired man could still be here in Yuma, could have stationed himself at the landing to check the departing steamboat passengers. But the other possibility was even more unsettling—that she'd taken it into her head to get shut of me after all, despite what she'd said last night. She was an unpredictable woman; the secrets she was harboring might have led her to change her mind about allowing me to accompany her north to Callville.

If that was the case, she wouldn't be boarding the upriver steamer. She'd know the boat would not leave before I got to the wharf; she couldn't escape me that way. Hell, I thought then, it could even be she'd never intended to take the *Mohave*. The cousin she claimed to have in Callville might be another lie, the passage she'd bought a ruse to hide her real destination from me. If it was San Francisco she'd been planning to go to all along, it would be simple enough to alter her passage from an upriver steamer to a downriver one that would take her to La Bomba, where she could transfer to one of the fast packets bound up the Pacific coast.

It angered me to think of her deceiving me that way. But I did not want to judge her prematurely. It could still be that she'd left early for the *Mohave,* and I would give her the benefit of the doubt until I got down there myself.

I left the hotel and went along First Street at a fast walk. To the east, the edge of the sun had risen above the distant mountains; the sky in that direction was awash with golden light. The town was just beginning to stir to life. Wagons rumbled on the dusty street; merchants were arriving to open their stores. From the river wharf I heard the first shrill blast of a steamer's whistle.

I turned on Main; Yuma Landing was at the end of that street, two blocks from a railroad bridge under construction. There were steamers tied up at two adjacent wharves, but more of the activity was centered on the one to my right, where the upriver sternwheeler, the *Mohave,* was moored. The downriver boat, at the left-hand wharf, was the smaller and older of the two; the *Mohave* was much more impressive.

The man in the Colorado Steam Navigation Company office last night had said she was the pride of the line. It was clear enough even from a distance that he'd had just cause for that claim. She was not as opulent as the Mississippi River packets—I'd ridden one of those during my fiddlefoot years before meeting Emma—but there was an elegance about her just the same. A hundred and fifty feet long and better than thirty feet abeam, she had three decks surmounted by a pilothouse and a pair of tall stacks. There was room aboard her for two hundred passengers, the steamship clerk had told me, and a hundred thousand pounds of cargo. And she was an engineering wonder in that she drew only thirty inches fully ballasted, which allowed her to glide fast and sure through the shallow waters of the Colorado, to winch herself over cascades in the narrow, rugged gorges far upriver.

Baggage vans and heavy freight wagons from the line of warehouses nearby clattered up the aft gangplank and onto the cargo deck, making the *Mohave* rock slightly against her mooring hawsers. White, Mexican, and Cocopah Indian roustabouts shouted curses in both English and Spanish, paying no mind to the women in the knots of gathering passengers. Astern, a long manila hawser stretched from the *Mohave*'s hog post to the towing bridle of a barge fenced all around except for a narrow gateway on the inboard side. The gap between the gate and the shore was bridged by a walled gangplank, and a crew of four troopers from Fort Yuma was prodding a line of army mules up the plank and into the barge.

The crowd milling about on the wharf was noisy, with that sense of excitement that seemed always to precede a steamer sailing. Bearded, rough-dressed miners bound for the gold camps upriver on the Arizona side; drummers and grifters and fiddlefoots; the wives of businessmen and military officers, and trollops on their way to parlor houses in La Paz and Ehrenberg and other towns. The only soldiers already in evidence were a major and a colonel in dress uniform, but as I approached I saw a company of cavalry marching down from the fort, barracks bags slung over their shoulders—replacements, probably, headed for Fort Mohave or one of the other back-country posts along the wild Arizona frontier.

I pushed my way through the throng on the wharf. None of the women was Jennifer Todd; none of the men had long yellow hair or a bushy red beard. At the top of the forward gangplank, a member of the *Mohave*'s crew stood by to answer questions and give directions. I took him for the purser, and he confirmed it when I climbed aboard and asked him.

"I'm looking for a woman named Jennifer Todd," I said, "bound for Callville." I described her. "Has she boarded yet?"

He shook his head. "Don't recall seeing anyone looked like that."

"She'd have arrived about a half hour ago."

"I've been here that long and more," he said. "Only a few passengers boarded that early. I'd remember if she was one of them."

"How long before departure?"

He took out his pocket watch, flicked the cover up. "Just about forty-five minutes."

I thanked him, and as I maneuvered back down the gangplank I kept a tight rein on my anger. It was still possible that Mrs. Todd had detoured off somewhere, that she would show up in time for the *Mohave*'s sailing. I decided to give her another few minutes before I went looking at the downriver boat. The idea that she had lied to me again, broken my trust, was one I did not want to accept.

I paced around near the gangplank, listening to the rumble of the boilers and the increasing hiss of exhaust steam audible above the din, alternately watching the crowd and the activity on and around the steamer. The last of the mules were driven onto the trailing barge, the gate closed and secured, and the plank drawn. The animals milled about for a time, then settled down to eating from racks of hay along either side or drinking from two big water puncheons at opposite corners. More freight wagons arrived, these laden with mining equipment. More passengers arrived, too, and began filing up the forward gangplank. But Jennifer Todd was not among them.

After no more than five minutes, my restlessness and anger were such that I couldn't wait any longer. I went along to the bank and out onto the adjacent wharf to where the downriver boat was tied up. There were fewer passengers there, not so much cargo being loaded. I climbed the gangplank and stopped in front of that packet's purser.

I told him who I was looking for, asked him if he'd seen her. And he said, "Yes, sir, I sure did. Pretty young woman. Came aboard about twenty-five minutes ago; had upriver passage, but said she'd changed her mind and wanted to go to La Bomba instead."

Tight-lipped, I said, "Did she ask for a stateroom?"

"She did."

"Which one did you give her?"

"Eight, starboard. But you won't find her there."

"Why not?"

"She's not on board. She left not two minutes after I spoke to her."

"Have you any idea where she went?"

"No, sir. Her and the gent with her headed back across the wharf. That was the last I saw of her."

My anger turned to alarm. The sudden tension knotted muscles, closed my hands into fists. "Do you know the man who was with her?"

"Never saw him before. He came on board just after she did. Caught up with her over by the stairway, talked to her some, and then they disembarked. She didn't look none too pleased about leaving, come to think of it."

"What did this man look like?"

"Well, he was a small fellow, rough-dressed, hadn't shaved in a while. Struck me he might be a miner."

"What color was his hair?"

"Yellow," the purser said. "Like General Custer's. Long yellow hair."

CHAPTER 14

I PIVOTED AWAY from him and ran down the gang-plank, almost bowling over a fat man just starting up with a war bag. I was angry clear through now—and scared clear through. No matter that Jennifer Todd had tried to deceive me; I had committed myself to protecting her, and she needed my help now more than she ever had. But Christ, where was she? Where had the yellow-haired man taken her? Twenty minutes had elapsed since he'd forced her to leave the steamer—she'd never have gone with him unless he'd showed her some kind of weapon, threatened her—and they could be anywhere by this time. They could be on their way out of Yuma.

She could be dead by this time.

That thought pulsed in my mind as I raced along the wharf, dodging wagons and animals, roustabouts and civilian passengers. It had me half panicked. If the yellow-haired man was Mase Todd, chances were he wouldn't harm her, not here in Yuma. But what if he wasn't Mase Todd? In that case I had no clear idea why he was after her, what his intentions were. For all I knew, his aim could be murder.

I cursed myself for having wasted time before I checked the downriver boat. And for not keeping a closer watch on Mrs. Todd. She had brought this on herself by not trusting me, by not paying enough heed to my warnings about the yellow-haired man being here in Yuma, but that didn't excuse the fact that I had failed her. If I couldn't find her, if I was too late . . .

When I reached the shore I slowed to a stop, fighting the panic, trying to make myself think clearly. Above, the town sprawled shimmering in the early-morning heat. Somewhere up there was Yuma's town marshal; but I did not know where, and even if I found him and explained the situation, there was little enough he could do without some idea of where the yellow-haired man had gone with Mrs. Todd.

Warehouses lined the riverbank, teamsters and stevedores flowing in and out of those with open doors. Fort Yuma loomed on its hill to the north; behind the warehouses to the south, clusters of sun-baked 'dobes and *jacales* marked the Mexican quarter. I doubted he would have taken her in the direction of the fort. The Mexican section, then? Or up the hill and into the town proper?

Damn it, *where?*

In front of the nearest south-side warehouse, a bean-pole of a man was shouting at a group of stevedores loading crates of mining equipment onto a dray wagon. I hastened over to him, thinking that he might have seen Mrs. Todd and the yellow-haired man pass by and noted where they'd gone. But he hadn't; he'd been too busy to pay attention to anyone, he said. I called out to the stevedores, but they only shook their heads.

A group of boys had gathered up on Main Street to watch the departure of the steamers; I recalled pass-

ing them on my way down to the wharf. I ran to where
they were tossing a ball back and forth.

"Did any of you see a man and a woman come by
here about a half hour ago?" I asked them. "The
woman was blond, carrying a carpetbag. The man had
long yellow hair."

The boys looked at me in silence for some mo-
ments. Then a towhead of about ten said diffidently,
"I did, mister."

I stepped toward him too quickly; he flinched away
from me. I made myself smile to put him at his ease.
"Which way did they go, son? It's important."

"They went over where the Mexs live," he said. "I
thought it was funny they'd do that; that's why I noticed."

"Did they stop anywhere?"

"I don't know, mister. I lost sight of 'em . . ."

I ran past the rear of the warehouses, down to where
the Mexican quarter straggled away to the south. Beyond the first row of 'dobes and *jacales,* a narrow
alley led uphill to a small plaza; I turned onto its dusty
ruts. An old woman in black, with a market basket
looped over her arm, was coming along the plaza. I
stopped in front of her, repeated my question about
the yellow-haired man and Mrs. Todd. She shook her
head to indicate that she didn't understand, didn't
speak English.

There was no one else in the plaza except for a
drunken Cocopah propped against the front wall of a
cantina. I ran past him, down another alley to the
south. At the corner where it intersected with a second uphill street, two young women in low-cut blouses
and flowered skirts were sitting in front of a large
'dobe building, eating tortillas and refried beans.
Putas, I thought when I saw the businesslike smiles
that appeared on their mouths; the building was probably a crib that catered to the teamsters and rivermen.

"Company, *señor?*" the younger of the two said. One of her front teeth was gold, and it gleamed an added invitation in the sun.

"Men who wish company before breakfast—such men they are, Estrellita," the other one said and giggled. *"¿No es verdad?"*

"I'm not looking for company," I snapped at them. "I'm looking for a blond woman and a small man with yellow hair. They were around here about twenty minutes ago."

The two *putas* lost interest. The younger one rolled her eyes and said, "Ai, gringos," and the older woman nodded in agreement.

"Did you see them?"

"And if I did, *señor?*"

"I've got to find them. The man abducted the woman; I think he might want to hurt her."

"Abducted?"

"Secuestrara," the other one translated.

"Ah. That is bad."

I fumbled in the pocket of my Levi's, found a silver dollar, and held it out where Estrellita could see it. "This is for you if you can tell me where they went."

Greed flickered in her eyes. She stood, set her plate on her chair, and moved to where she could look down to the river. She lifted her arm. "That building there, *señor.* You see it?"

She was pointing toward a tumbledown structure a hundred yards distant, set well back from the river's edge and surrounded by mud flats. It looked to be an abandoned warehouse; part of its timbered roof had caved in at the rear.

I said, "They went inside there?"

"Sí. She does not wish to go inside, the blond woman; she struggles." Estrellita shrugged, and the

gold tooth flashed again. "I think they are lovers," she said.

"Love before breakfast," the older whore said. "That is how you yourself came to be a *puta,* eh, Estrellita?"

I tossed the silver dollar to Estrellita and pounded down toward the warehouse. The fear had set up a throbbing in my head; my mouth was coppery with the taste of it. The yellow-haired man wouldn't have taken Jennifer to a place like that unless he meant to do her harm. And he'd had more than fifteen minutes alone in there with her . . .

I drew my .44 as I neared the building, forced myself to slow in order to keep my balance on the muddy ground. When I came around the front corner I could see that one of the two double doors stood partway open. I moved in close to the wall, started toward the door.

And the yellow-haired man walked out through the open doorway, carrying Jennifer's carpetbag in one hand.

He was looking in my direction and he saw me in the same instant. He dodged back inside, his free hand dropping to his holstered pistol. I fired at him, missed high in my haste; the bullet sent adobe chips flying from the wall. I was still carrying my saddlebags draped over my left shoulder and I reached up and pulled them off, flung them down as I ran ahead to the door. When I flattened back next to it I could hear the scrape of his boots from the semidarkness inside: He was moving away from the door, fast. All I could think of was Jennifer; I lunged around the jamb and threw myself into the warehouse, hit hard-packed earth, and rolled to the left.

Two shots erupted, echoing off the 'dobe walls, but neither of them found me. I came up on my knees, with my pistol extended at arm's length. He was over near a jumble of timbers and bricks from the collapsed roof; sunlight streaming down through the gap let me see him clearly. I fired again just as he squeezed off for the third time. His bullet slashed past my head; mine took him somewhere in the body and pitched him sideways into the debris. But it didn't finish him. On his knees, trailing his left arm, he scrambled behind one of the timbers.

The rotting remains of several empty crates were stacked haphazardly to my left; I dropped flat and crawled into their cover before he could use his pistol again. The warehouse floor stank of the river, of the manure of rats. I rubbed sweat out of my eyes, peered around one of the crates. I couldn't see the yellow-haired man, but I could see the carpetbag where he'd dropped it. And I could see something else, too, thirty feet away from where he was hidden.

It was Jennifer Todd, lying asprawl on the dirt floor, face down and unmoving.

I went wild inside. Without thinking, my lips skinned in against my teeth, I moved on hands and knees to the far end of the stack and then raised up to my feet and charged forward, firing. My first three shots were nowhere close to the yellow-haired man, but they kept him pinned down behind the timber until I got to where I could see where he was crouched. He sent one shot at me then, but he was wounded and his aim was off; he let out a yell and tried to twist away, cutting loose again as he made his lunge.

I shot him twice at twenty paces.

The bullets flung him over onto his side, then onto his back across a pile of bricks. His fingers relaxed and his pistol skittered loose; he didn't move. I knew he was dead even as I stepped up close to him. His eyes were open, staring sightlessly at the patch of sky visible through the collapsed section of roof.

My hands began to tremble. I jammed my pistol

into its holster, turned away from him, and ran to where Jennifer lay. Kneeling beside her, I probed at the artery in her neck—and felt the low, steady rhythm of her pulse. She was unconscious, not dead, and it didn't look as though she'd been shot. Through the spread fan of her hair, I could see a fresh bruise at the nape of her neck.

Relief washed through me, slackened the tension in my body, and left me feeling weak. I turned her, lifted her into a sitting position against my leg, and chafed her hands and face. After a time she groaned. The muscles around her eyes rippled; then the eyes popped open, and at first they were blind with terror. She struggled against me, tried to claw free of my grasp.

"Jennifer, it's all right, it's Roy Boone."

The sound of my voice calmed her. Her eyes focused on me: some of the terror faded out of them. "Roy, thank God! That man, the one with the yellow hair . . . he kidnapped me from the wharf, he attacked me. . . ."

"Easy now, it's done with."

"But he stole my carpetbag! We've got to find him. . . ."

"Your bag's right here," I said. "So is he."

She sat up, saw me looking past her, and turned her head to follow my gaze. Then she shuddered, and the tension went out of her body as it had gone out of mine. Her eyes shifted to me again. "Did you . . . ?"

"Yes," I said, "I killed him. It was almost the other way around."

"Praise God it wasn't." She winced, reached up to touch the bruise on her neck. "But how did you find me? I thought—" She broke off, looked down at her dust-streaked skirts.

"I know what you thought," I said. "I talked to the purser on the downriver steamer; he told me you'd asked to change your passage to La Bomba. He also told me you'd left with the yellow-haired man. I found some people who saw where he took you. He was just leaving when I got here."

"Roy . . . I'm sorry. I didn't want to deceive you. . . ."

"Then why did you?"

"I can't explain, not now. It was something I felt I had to do, that's all."

I lifted my chin toward the dead man across the warehouse floor. "Who was he?"

"I don't know. I never saw him before today."

"Is that the truth?"

"Yes. I swear it."

"I thought he might be your husband," I said.

"Mase? God, no."

"What did he say when he accosted you on the boat?"

She hesitated. Then she said, "That he was a friend of Mase's and was going to take me back to the ranch. He had a weapon; he said he'd use it if I tried to call for help. I had no choice, I had to go with him. But then he brought me here. I don't know why . . ."

"You're lying," I said.

She shook her head. "I'm not."

"You're lying," I repeated flatly. "You know why he brought you here. I think maybe I do, too. He was after your carpetbag, wasn't he? That is what he's been after all along."

The fear in her seemed to deepen. She pushed away from me, got unsteadily to her feet. I let her take two steps toward where the carpetbag lay before I stood, too, and moved past her and caught up the bag myself.

She said anxiously. "Let me have it."

"No."

"It's mine . . ."

"The bag, yes. Not what's inside."

"What . . . what are you going to do?"

"I haven't decided yet. Right now we're going to get out of here."

Jennifer glanced over at the body of the yellow-haired man lying blood-spattered in the rubble, and another shudder passed through her. I kept my gaze on her face; I did not want to look at death again. I had killed men in the war, but that had been a long time ago, and it had filled me with loathing. The loathing was the same now, even though I had had just cause to take the yellow-haired man's life.

Without speaking, she pivoted toward the open door, still a little unsteady on her feet. I moved up beside her, and we went out into the bright sunlight and the gathering heat. There was no one in the vicinity, no one visible anywhere closer than in the Mexican section uphill. If anybody had heard the shooting—and I thought the two *putas* must have—they had ignored it, the way most people did in frontier towns like Yuma.

I bent to pick up my saddlebags. From over at the landing, a steamer's whistle echoed sharply as I straightened again. Jennifer started, then turned to face me. "The boats," she said. "Roy, they haven't left yet!"

"They will any minute."

"We can still get aboard if we hurry."

"We? Now you want me to go with you, is that it?"

"Please, Roy." Her eyes were as imploring as her voice. "I don't want to stay in Yuma."

"Why not? The man who was after you and your carpetbag is dead."

"Mase isn't dead," she said. "For all we know, he's here too. You said that yourself."

"Your husband is the redhead with the beard, isn't he?"

"Yes. I should have told you that before. But I—"

The steamer's whistle sounded again. Urgently, she caught hold of my arm. "For God's sake, please. We have to hurry!"

"Jennifer, what you did is wrong. Don't you understand that? But you can make it right again."

"How?"

"Come with me to the local law. That's the proper thing to do—"

"No," she said.

"I killed that man in there. I can't just leave him here without reporting it."

"No," Jennifer said again. "I won't go willingly to the law. I won't stay here in Yuma."

"If I let you leave, it will be without the carpetbag."

She looked at me a moment longer, her face twisted with emotion; then she spun and began to run toward the wharves. I chased after her, the carpetbag a heavy weight in my right hand. I was certain of what was in it now and just as certain that my duty was to take it, and Jennifer Todd, to the Yuma marshal. Yet I could not bring myself to take hold of her, pull her away with me into town. Her panic was genuine; she wanted desperately to leave Yuma. And perhaps she had a right to that much. Not to the carpetbag and what it contained, but to her freedom. And no matter what she'd done, I still felt protective toward her.

I ran at her side, not speaking, trying to come to a decision. When we emerged between two of the warehouses I saw that the downriver steamer had begun moving away from its wharf. But the *Mohave* was still tied up at the one adjacent. It appeared as though there was time for Jennifer to reach it—time for me to reach it with her.

We passed the warehouse nearest the foot of Main Street. I slowed when we got to the wharf; she ran ahead a few paces, then her stride faltered and she swung her head around. "Roy!" When I didn't answer she plunged forward again, headlong down the wharf toward the *Mohave*.

Let her go, I thought. Take the carpetbag to the marshal, get shut of her for good. That is what she wanted all along, isn't it?

But I couldn't do it. The thought that if I allowed her to go I might never see her again was somehow painful. I could not abandon her now, not like this, not with questions still unanswered; and I knew I couldn't just coldly reveal her to the law, either. Right or wrong, I was still bound to her—a bond I wasn't sure I wanted, a bond that scared me, but a bond just the same.

I pounded after her along the wharf. Two Cocopah deckhands were preparing to ship the forward gangplank; Jennifer waved her arms, calling out, and they paused and then held it in place. I was right behind her as she flung herself up on deck.

Seconds later, the gangplank was free of the wharf, and the *Mohave* was under way.

CHAPTER 15

WITH A RUSH of churning water, the big stern paddle wheel began its splashing rhythm. The *Mohave* quivered as she nosed away from the wharf. The towing hawser from the hog post to the mule barge astern tightened, jerking the barge into movement; the strong current slid it sideways until the towing bridle took control and brought it around, straightening it into line. The beat of the boilers, the thud of the walking beam engine, the hissing of steam were punctuated by another sharp blast from the pilothouse whistle.

Jennifer stood at the hammock-netted rail, catching her breath. I was right beside her, but she would not look at me; her gaze was on the barge astern. There was no sign of the purser on the cargo deck, and after a couple of minutes I maneuvered Jennifer through the soldiers and deck passengers lining the rail, up the aft stairway to the Texas deck.

We found the purser in the ship's office. He showed no sign of recognition when I asked which staterooms had been assigned to Mrs. Todd and me;

he seemed to have forgotten our conversation earlier, and Jennifer had not talked to him about canceling her passage. Our rooms were adjoining, it turned out—numbers 9 and 10 on the starboard side, facing the Arizona shore.

When we came out on deck again, the strip of muddy, foam-flecked water between the boat and the shore had widened considerably, and we were nearing midstream. My hand on Jennifer's arm again, I guided her down the stairway to the cabin deck and into the tunnel down its center.

"We'll talk in my stateroom," I said as we neared the door marked with the brass numeral 9.

She said nothing; she hadn't spoken a word since we'd boarded. She seemed relieved now, but in a resigned way, as if whatever had sustained her these past few days had deserted her. I thought I knew what it was, just as I knew what I would find when I opened her carpetbag.

The cabin was small, eight feet by ten, and already hot. On the aft bulkhead were two bunks, one above the other. Opposite on the forward bulkhead was a bolted-down stand with a tin basin inside its sunken top that would drain into a pipe running below deck and emptying into the river; secured behind a wooden rack on top was a metal pitcher of water. There was nothing else in the room except for a heavy louvered door in the side bulkhead.

Jennifer sat on the lower bunk, swept her hair back to finger the bruise on her neck. I put the carpetbag and my saddlebags on the washstand and then opened the louvered door to let in the breeze that blew in small, hot gusts across the river. Outside, thick planks formed barriers to the left and right so that each cabin had a small, private section of deck. I could see that the wharves and warehouses, the fort and the territorial prison and the rest of Yuma had

fallen away astern. The *Mohave* was entering the
outer curve of the first bend, and there was nothing
to see ahead but lowlands covered with underbrush
and arrowweed, the sunblasted flats and dry-rock hills
of the gallows land beyond.

I turned to face Jennifer again. She hadn't moved
from the bunk; her hands were in her lap now, rubbing against each other with a dry, scraping sound.
She did not look at me as I stepped back to the washstand and opened the carpetbag.

It contained what I had known it would: my spare
pistol, the one she claimed to have lost in the desert;
and wrapped in articles of clothing at the bottom,
several banded stacks of greenbacks and a half-dozen
leather pouches that would be filled with gold dust.

An odd sort of sorrow came into me. I said, "The
money in here belongs to the territorial bank in Maricopa Wells. It says so on the bands around the greenbacks."

She raised her head. "I didn't know it was stolen
when I took it. I swear to you I didn't."

"You must have had some idea."

"But I didn't *know*. I . . . didn't want to know."

"Where did you get it?"

"The man I shot at the ranch, the one who attacked me—it was in his saddlebags."

"Did you know that before you shot him?"

"No. Do you think I killed him for the money?
My God, Roy, I'm not that kind."

"I didn't think anything," I said. "I only want the
truth."

"I've told you the truth about what happened that
night. The only thing I didn't tell you about was the
money."

"Why did you take it? Why didn't you turn it over
to the sheriff in Maricopa Wells?"

"I told you, I didn't know it was stolen. I thought

it might be, but . . . it could have belonged to him,
it could have been his life savings that he'd drawn
out of the bank."

"He could have had kin, too—a family that needed
that money."

"You can't make me feel any more guilty than I
already do," she said. "But I was terrified that night;
I'd killed a man, and Mase might come home at any
second. The money . . . it was more money than I'd
ever seen or hoped to see. I didn't know what to do
at first. But then I thought that if it was stolen, Mase
might have had a hand in the theft. If I gave the
money to the sheriff, Mase would kill me. And I
couldn't just wait and give it to him, with that dead
man lying in the yard; I couldn't, Roy."

"So you decided to run away with it."

"Don't you understand? I saw it as my only chance
to escape from Mase, from that desert ranch—my
only chance to make a new life for myself. I *had* to
do it."

"I understand," I said. "But it's stolen money, Jennifer. What kind of new life would it be for you with
money others have sweated and toiled for? Do you
really think you'd have been able to forget how you
got it, that your conscience would have let you forget?"

"It's easy for you to judge me—you're a man, and
a man can make his way in this country. But it's not
the same for a woman alone, unless she has money
to see her through."

"That doesn't change the fact that this money is
not yours to keep."

She was silent for several seconds. Then she said
in a low voice, "What are you going to do?"

"About you? Nothing. You needn't worry that I'll
make trouble for you with the law."

"And the money? What about that?"

"I can't let you keep it. I'll take it to the ship's office and have the purser lock it in his safe. When we get to the first of the upriver towns I'll leave this boat, take the downriver steamer when it comes, and hand the money over to the law in Yuma. You can come with me or not; that's up to you. If not, I'll explain what happened as best I can."

"I've never known a man like you," she said. "Are you truly so principled?"

"I don't know. All I know is, a man does what he feels he has to."

"A woman does, too. But women are more realistic. They can bend with the circumstances."

"Even if it means doing wrong?"

"Roy, without that money, I have nothing. Can't you see that?"

"No," I said, "I can't, because it's not true. You have your self-respect, you have your future—"

"What future do I have?" she said bitterly.

"You don't need to abandon your dream. You can still realize it."

"How? By becoming a saloon girl, a trollop? How else could a woman like me make enough money to open a boardinghouse?"

"Why do you underestimate yourself? Jennifer, you're a decent woman—you're an intelligent woman. You can still go to San Francisco, find a respectable job—"

"I can't."

"Why can't you?"

"Because I have almost no money of my own. I told you the truth about that Mason jar Mase kept buried in the corral. But there was only forty dollars in it."

"Then the stage fare and the passage to Callville came out of the bank's money?"

"Yes."

"All right. I'll replace it for you when the time comes; I have enough cash left to cover it."

"You'd do that for me, after all the trouble I've caused you? Why?"

"I'm not exactly sure. Maybe it's just that I feel sorry for you."

"I don't need anyone to feel sorry for me. I don't want pity, not from you or anyone else."

The way she said that made me aware again of her pride, of that odd mixture of strength and vulnerability. She'd survived against odds that would have killed most women. And then she had thought she'd found the way to make her dream come true, only to lose it again. Still, it was the wrong path she'd chosen because it was one built on falsehood and theft; perhaps someday she'd come to realize that, accept the fact that I was keeping her from making another serious mistake in her life.

I said, "I don't pity you. I'm only sorry for what you've been through. You can pay me back when you get settled in with your cousin in Callville."

She averted her gaze, stared down at her hands.

"Or don't you have a cousin in Callville?" I said.

"No, I don't. I . . . I lied about that, too."

"Well, I figured you had. So you could slip away from me this morning and take the downriver steamer, isn't that right?"

"Yes. But I—" She broke off and shook her head. "It doesn't really matter anymore, does it?"

"It matters," I said. "The thing about lies is that if you tell enough of them, they become a habit, an easy way to avoid responsibility."

"You needn't preach to me."

"I'm not. Do you know anyone in Callville or any of the upriver towns?"

"No."

"So it's pointless for you to stay on this boat."

"I have nowhere else to go," she said.

"There is still San Francisco."

Her head lifted. "How can I go to San Francisco without money?"

"The same way you were planning to this morning. Exchange your Callville passage for passage to the coast. There will be a difference in the price, but I can take care of that for you, too. We can both disembark at the first town and wait there together for the downriver boat."

"We?"

"I'll see you safe to San Francisco, if you want me to," I said.

"You'd still do that, too?"

"Only if it's what you want."

"I . . . I don't know . . ."

"Think on it, then. It will be at least a day before we come to a town; there's plenty of time for you to make a decision."

I took the greenbacks and dust pouches out of the carpetbag, then emptied one of my saddlebags and put the money in there. When I looked at Jennifer again her eyes had a dull sheen and her face was heavy with resignation.

She said softly, "What do you want from me, Roy?"

"I don't want anything from you."

"Men always want something from a woman."

I could feel my mouth tighten at the corners. "Is that what you've come to think of me? That I expect your favors in return for my help?"

"I don't know what to think anymore . . ."

"Well, you can get that dauncy idea straight out of your head." Anger made the words come out sharp. "You asked me not to judge you; I'll thank you not to make judgments about me, either. Not all men are like your husband, Jennifer. Not all men are sons-of-bitches."

I caught up the saddlebag with the money in it, went out without looking at her again, and shut the door quietly behind me.

CHAPTER 16

A BELL BEGAN to ring, announcing breakfast in the main salon, as I came out of the ship's office. Passengers were already gathering, all of them civilians; the soldiers would have their own mess on the cargo deck. I gave no thought to joining the line. Food was the last thing I wanted just now.

I went instead to the saloon. It bore no resemblance to the elegant cardrooms of the Mississippi River packets; it was an oblong room with a low ceiling, several plain tables, and a mahogany counter behind which were racks of bottles and glasses and a heavy-set barkeep in a striped shirt. The only other man in the room was sitting at one of the rear tables, laying out a solitaire board; I marked him as a gambler because of his brocade vest and the green sleeve garters that held shirt cuffs away from his wrists. He gave me a speculative look as I entered, but when I showed no interest he returned his attention to the layout of cards.

I crossed to the bar counter. "Coffee," I said to the heavy-set man. "And a shot of whiskey."

The pot of coffee had been freshly delivered from the galley; the muddy-looking brew was still steaming. When the barkeep set the glass of whiskey in front of me he said conversationally, "Hair of the dog?"

"No."

"Thought it might be. You don't mind my saying so, mister, you look a mite rumpled this morning."

I killed a man this morning, I thought. But I said only, "What do I owe you?"

He shrugged and told me, and I paid him. Then I carried the coffee and the whiskey to one of the empty tables, away from where the gambler was sitting. From the chair I slumped into I could look out through the windows at the Arizona shore, the gallows land wrapped in heat haze beyond the brush-strewn river-bank. Empty, desolate—the same as I felt inside.

Part of the emptiness was the yellow-haired man, lying dead with three of my bullets in him back in Yuma. Killing came easy to some, but not to me; each time I had been forced to kill a man during the war, a small portion of me had died too, and it was the same this time. It made no difference that it had been done in self-defense. Life was too precious to me, especially now, after losing Emma, to take it from someone—even an outlaw—without a feeling of sadness and remorse.

The other part of the emptiness was Jennifer Todd. And it was less simple to understand. I kept telling myself there was nothing personal in my attitude toward her, and yet if that was true, why did all her lies and improper behavior feel like a betrayal? And why did I stand ready even now to go on protecting her all the way to San Francisco?

I remembered what Frank Rhodes had said to me about her at the way station: *"Man gets so he can judge people, women in particular. She ain't a bad one, Mr. Boone."* Well, she wasn't. Maybe that was the reason it disappointed and fretted me, all the things she'd done; the reason why I kept wanting to help her.

But maybe there was more to it than that, something lodged and growing inside me, something I did not want to admit because I was afraid of it. I knew the word for that something, but I wouldn't let myself think it. Not now. Not for a long time to come, if ever.

I drank some of the whiskey, forcing my thoughts to settle on the series of events back in Maricopa Wells and at the Todd ranch that had entangled my life with Jennifer's—the truth I had been after the past several days. I thought I knew now what had happened, or at least most of it. It must have gone something like this:

The bank in Maricopa Wells had been robbed by Mase Todd, the yellow-haired man, and the big fellow I'd later found dead at the Todd ranch. After they rode out of town, they'd split up in three different directions to confuse the posse. Todd had circled back into Maricopa Wells and joined the posse himself; he was known there, and he'd been masked during the robbery, so doing that wouldn't have been difficult for him. The idea had probably been for Todd to maneuver the posse onto a false trail to ensure that the other two made good their escape. Then the three of them could meet later, at a prearranged place—the Todd ranch—to make their split.

The third fellow had been the one carrying the bank loot. Only he'd made the mistake of getting himself liquored up before riding to the ranch, and when he got there he'd made the further mistake of trying to attack Jennifer. She'd shot him, then found the money and run with it. After she was gone, the yellow-haired man arrived and discovered the big one dead and the money gone. He'd still been there when I showed up. He was the one who had been hidden in the pulque cactus and who'd clubbed me with the pole, who'd searched my saddlebags while I was unconscious; he hadn't known why I was there, and he must have thought at first that I might have the stolen money. He was also the one who had ransacked the ranchhouse and who'd set out after Jennifer when he found her tracks leading through the draw. He'd figured by then that she was the one who had made off with the money.

The reason why the posse had shown up at the ranch the next morning was unclear. Maybe Mase Todd hadn't been able to misdirect them as planned, and they'd managed to follow the big one's trail, or the yellow-haired man's; that seemed the most likely explanation. Todd had been as surprised as the others to discover his confederate's body and Jennifer gone. But he'd also realized what must have happened, and as soon as he could separate himself from the posse, he'd ridden out on his own to search for her and for the yellow-haired man.

Todd hadn't found Jennifer, and neither had yellowhair, but they'd run across each other somewhere on the desert, probably on El Camino Real del Diablo. They must have concluded that she'd headed west toward Yuma, and they'd been hunting her when they encountered me at the water tank. The yellow-haired one had recognized me and jumped to the conclusion that I was also looking for Jennifer; that was why he and Todd had tried to kill me that night.

What had happened after I'd escaped the arroyo and run off their horses was also unclear. It could be they had had some sort of falling out, as I'd felt to be a possibility before, and yellow-hair had killed Mase Todd and come on to Yuma alone. If that was the case, then neither Jennifer nor I had anything more to fear. But it could also be that they'd split up again, with Todd riding off in another direction to search for Jennifer; it was a logical decision for them to have made, because they hadn't any idea where she was headed. If Mase Todd was still alive, then her life— and mine, as long as I stayed with her—was potentially still in danger. The sooner we got clear of the gallows land and on our way to San Francisco, the better it would be for both of us.

I finished the whiskey, washed it down with coffee, and went over to the bar counter again. As upset as I had been earlier, I had neglected to ask the purser how long it would be before we reached the nearest settlement, but I thought that the barkeep would know. And he did.

"Current's running fast," he said. "We'll make three—four miles an hour going up, with Captain Mellon at the wheel. That should put us into Dent's Landing sometime tomorrow morning."

"Captain Jack Mellon?"

"None other."

Jack Mellon was a legend on the Colorado River. He had steamed its length back and forth for a decade and a half, and it was said he knew it better than any man alive. If the stories I had heard about him were true, he had once dug up a three-hundred-pound anchor buried in a mudflat and carried it back to his ship without assistance. In his hands, the *Mohave* was a safe boat to travel on despite the treacherous waters of the Colorado.

I asked, "What sort of settlement is Dent's Landing? Is it a town or a mining camp?"

"Just a camp. Not much there except a few shacks and a general store."

Which meant that there would be no accommodations for anyone waiting for a downriver steamer, and a rough bunch living there. "What would be the first town of any size we come to?" I asked.

"Well, that would be Ehrenberg. There's Cibola, but you'd hardly call it a town."

Ehrenberg was the shipping point for the inland Apache-fighting garrisons, the place where the company of cavalry and the barge of army mules would leave the *Mohave*. There would be accommodations there; it would be the safest spot for Jennifer and me to disembark with the money.

"How soon will we reach Ehrenberg?"

"Day after tomorrow, likely," the barkeep said. "Depends on the current."

I thanked him, shook my head at his query for another drink—one whiskey was all I had wanted; any more in the mounting heat would fuddle my mind—and went out to pass time on the decks.

The day and the miles wore on with the same heat-soaked slowness as they had on the Butterfield stage.

There was little enough to do on the riverboat; the two main pastimes, aside from meals, were conversation and gambling, and I was interested in neither of those. But I did have freedom of movement, at least. I climbed to the Texas deck and watched a Cocopah deckhand, out on the bow with a long pole, take regular channel soundings and shout word back to the pilothouse of any freshly formed sandbars or unexpected snags to be avoided. When it got too hot up there I descended to the cargo deck, where there was shade, and listened to the replacement soldiers banter with each other. Most of them were young, a few little more than boys, and on their faces was the same eagerness that had been on mine when I joined the Union Army during the war. That would change soon enough, once they got into Apache country, once they tasted hardship and terror and death. I knew what their faces would be like then—those that survived and those that didn't.

Toward noon, one of the troopers, a wizened fellow wearing a sergeant's stripes, used a pulley rig hooked onto the towing hawser to slide back to the barge. He filled the water puncheons by lowering a rope-tied bucket to the river and then stirred the mules to give them a small measure of exercise. Watching him do those things, and a pair of Cocopahs bring him back to the *Mohave* by means of a rope attached to the pulley rig, passed another half hour for me.

I still had little appetite, but when the bell rang to announce the noon meal I went up to the main salon, stood in line, and eventually took a seat at the purser's table. Jennifer was not among the gathered passengers and crew, and it was just as well that she wasn't. It seemed we had already said all there was to say to each other, at least for this day; and seeing her would only have deepened the emptiness inside me.

After the meal, with its polite shipboard talk that I listened to but did not join, I returned to the cargo deck. It was scorching hot by this time, close to a hundred degrees in the shade, I judged, and most of the soldiers were sitting silently among the hogsheads and crates and other goods lashed to the deck. But this heat was nothing compared to what it would be like out here in July and August, when temperatures would rise to a hundred twenty degrees and higher. I remembered my father telling me of one upriver trip he'd made at that time of year; they had had to cover their waterbags with dampened flannel, he'd said, then hang them in the shade in order to keep the water cool enough to drink.

Some past three o'clock, a sandstorm whipped up off the Arizona desert and covered the boat and everyone on it in gritty yellow dust. I went to my cabin and took a sponge bath and beat the dust out of my clothes. Then I lay on the upper bunk and let the boat's motion and the rhythmic chunk of the paddle wheel put me to sleep for a time, until the supper bell rang in the main salon.

When I entered the salon a few minutes later, Jennifer was there, seated at the first officer's table, looking solemn and unhappy. Our eyes met as I passed, but she averted hers immediately, as if she felt embarrassed, or perhaps ashamed. I went on past and sat again at the purser's table, with my back to her, and did not turn around as I ate boiled beef, canned vegetables, and fresh biscuits. By the time I finished and left the salon, Jennifer was gone. Back to her cabin, probably; I did not see her anywhere as I roamed about the steamer.

A half hour before sundown, Captain Mellon found a place for us to lay over for the night—a wide backwater created by the shifting course of the river, at the apex of a long curve toward the California side. Bells rang and the paddle wheel slowed to a stop, so that the *Mohave* was moving only with the current as she approached the mouth of the backwater. Then the whistle sounded and bells rang again and the huge wheel churned in reverse, acting as a brake. The boat and the river fought each other for two or three minutes, like the old enemies they were; but finally the *Mohave* pulled free, with a forward thrust of power, and slid herself and the mule barge crosscurrent into the backwater's long, placid length.

Two Cocopah deckhands jumped ashore to make the lines fast. As soon as the boat was secure and the engines shut down, the rest of the Indians fled in a bunch, carrying bedrolls and provisions, and disappeared into the underbrush and arrowweed that grew to the water's edge. Their fear of the river at night and of the demons they believed to be hidden in its mists was as strong as any fundamentalist Christian's fear of hellfire and damnation.

Sunset reddened the sky and the silent, twisting surface of the Colorado. The desert shadows lengthened, and as night began to close down, the wind blew cool again. I stood on the lee side of the pilothouse, alone, smoking my corncob, and watched the last of the red fade out like old dye on the western horizon. I wasn't thinking much; I hadn't since this morning in the saloon. It was an evening made for quiet enjoyment, and there was little enough that brought me pleasure these days.

Full dark had settled, with the moon painting everything in silver again, when Jennifer found me. Because of the steady pulse of voices in the saloon and main salon, I didn't hear her until she said, "Hello, Roy," from a few feet away. When I turned toward her the moonlight showed me the same solemn expression she had worn at supper.

"It's a nice night, isn't it," she said.

"Yes, it is."

"Do you mind if I stand here with you for a while?"

My pipe had gone out; I put it into the pocket of my coat. "Suit yourself."

"I don't blame you if you're still angry with me . . ."

"I'm not angry," I said. "Not anymore."

She was silent for a time, looking out at the dark river and the desert beyond. I sensed there was something she wanted to say; she wouldn't have sought me out otherwise. I waited for her to get it said.

It took her two or three minutes. Then, in a low voice, "I want to apologize."

"For what? For taking the bank's money?"

"For that, yes, and for lying to you back in Yuma. And for all the trouble I've caused you."

I didn't speak.

"I've done a lot of thinking since this morning," she said. "I . . . well, I feel differently now than I did then—I feel ashamed. I had no right to take that money; I'm sorry I did. The only decent thing is to give it back to the people it belongs to."

"Do you mean that? Or is it just another lie?"

"No, I can't lie to you anymore, and I won't. I mean it. I do, Roy."

The words sounded honest, heavy with feeling. I looked at her, a small, pale shape in the moonlit darkness, and I felt myself softening inside. "Then I'm glad," I said. "It will make things easier between us."

"I hope so." Pause. "You will still accompany me to San Francisco, won't you?"

"Yes. I told you I would, if it's what you want."

"It is. I don't want—" She broke off.

"You don't want what?"

"I don't want to run away from you anymore."

There was a kind of intimacy in those words, a meaning deeper than what they seemed on the surface. An awkwardness came into me; I moved away from her, over to the rail. After a moment she joined me, standing close—so close I could feel the nearness of her body, smell the sachet she wore and the woman scent of her hair.

"Just after Mase bought the ranch," she said, slow, "one of our neighbors gave me a puppy, a little terrier. Mase hated that poor animal; he mistreated it every chance he had, and it would cower and whimper every time he came near it. It became so afraid that it would cower when I came near it, too; once it even tried to bite me. It stopped trusting anyone, even the one person who cared for it."

Again I didn't speak.

"Mase shot it one morning," she said. "He found it digging in the corn patch and he just . . . he killed it. First he killed my love for him and then he killed

the only other thing I had to love. I swore I wouldn't
let myself love anything or anyone else, so I couldn't
be hurt that way again."

"What are you trying to say, Jennifer?"

"Don't you understand? That's why I tried to run
away from you back in Yuma. It wasn't that I was
afraid you would find out about the money; it was
that I was afraid of *you,* of what I was starting to feel
for you."

"I don't know what you mean—"

"But you do. You feel the same way about me. I've
known it since that first morning on the stage."

"No," I said.

"Yes. You're afraid of it, just as I was. You've only
just lost a woman you loved very much, and I've only
just lost a man I hated; we're both alone, running
away from the past and uneasy about the future. But
it doesn't have to be that way anymore. I've been
thinking about that all day too. I've admitted my feelings; if you do the same, it will be a relief for us both
and we can go on from there. We can, Roy, if you
want it to be that way."

I couldn't find words to say. I just stood stiff and
still, staring down at the patterns of light the *Mohave*'s
lamps made on the water; in places, it seemed as if
the surface was on fire.

Jennifer touched my arm. "Look at me, Roy," she
said.

I straightened from the rail and turned toward her.
Her eyes held mine; neither of us moved or spoke for
half a minute. I knew what was about to happen, and
I wanted it and didn't want it in equal measures, but
I was powerless to stop it. Then she said my name
again and came up against me, and my arms were
around her, and the embrace seemed strange, wrong,
and yet natural and right at the same time. Our mouths
joined, clumsily at first, then with more sureness, and

finally with hunger—on her part as well as mine. I tightened my arms around her, felt her caress my back and the nape of my neck. But only briefly; her hands released me and she brought them up between us, flat against my chest, and gently pushed me away.

For a moment she stood peering up at my face. Then she said, "I'd better go now. Think about what I've said. Good night, Roy."

Again I had no words. I just nodded, and she turned into the shadows on the other side of the pilothouse. Seconds later I heard the faint thump of her boots on the staircase.

I leaned against the rail. I couldn't seem to think clearly; I felt shaken and it was not just Jennifer's kiss, or the words she'd spoken, that were responsible. It was all the feelings new and old, all the uncertainties tumbling together inside of me, too.

Emma, I thought.

God, Emma, I don't know what to do.

CHAPTER 17

THE SHIP'S ENGINEERING crew fired the boilers at daybreak, the whistle sounded, and the massive paddle
wheel began to pummel the water again. Before the
dawn's flush faded into daylight, Captain Mellon had
the *Mohave* out into the main channel and once more
headed upriver.

I stood forward on the Texas deck, where I had
been for an hour or so, smoking and watching the
river mists crawl through the arrowweed on the banks
and then vanish like phantoms. There had been almost
no sleep for me during the night—I'd been up and
about since before four o'clock—and I felt logy and
sandy-eyed. And for all the restless thinking I had done,
I still did not know what to do. I seemed to want Jennifer and not want her in equal measures, the way I
had wanted and not wanted her kiss last night. A decision had to be made, and soon, but I just did not
seem able to make it yet.

Some past sunup, the bell sounded for breakfast.
The prospect of facing Jennifer this morning was dis-
quieting, and yet avoiding her was folly. Instead of

delaying, I went down immediately and knocked on the door to her cabin.

The awkwardness was in me again, but there was none in her. Her fine eyes held steady on mine when she opened the door, and the first thing she said was, "About last night, Roy—I won't apologize for what I said or did."

"You don't have to."

"Are you sorry it happened?"

"No, I don't think I am."

"But you're not sure?"

"I'm not sure of anything right now."

"It's all right," she said. "There's time, plenty of time. It won't happen again unless you want it to."

There was nothing more either of us cared to say. She took my arm, and we went into the main salon and took breakfast at the purser's table. His name was Brody, I had learned yesterday, and he was in high spirits this morning; he told stories of the river, and of Captain Mellon's exploits, and of other pilots he'd known in the early days of Colorado steamboating. His garrulous mood made it easier for me, and perhaps for Jennifer, because it allowed me to eat mostly in silence.

After the meal was done, I walked Jennifer back to her cabin. She was tired, she said—it was plain from the look of her that she hadn't had much sleep last night either—and she wanted to rest before the day's heat made the cabins unfit for occupancy. We agreed to meet later for the noon meal, and I left her and went out on deck again.

The *Mohave* was approaching her first stop, the settlement of Dent's Landing. There was not much to it, I saw—just a small landing, a freighting station corral attached to a general store, a saloon, and a scattering of ugly gray shacks and 'dobes. Behind it, a dusty road led away into the shimmering vastness of the desert. The settlement would supply the few silver and gold mines in the foothills nearby and provide a place for miners to drink bad whiskey and tequila once or twice a month.

The appearance of Dent's Landing, and of the rough crowd of men waiting at the landing, held no interest for me. I wandered up to the saloon and watched the gambler I'd seen yesterday take several dollars in gold specie and greenbacks from two drummers and a half-drunk miner. If the gambler was cheating, he was very good at his trade; I watched closely each time he dealt the cards, and each hand he played, and I couldn't detect any fancy maneuvers he might have made.

Evidently there was not much freight consigned to Dent's Landing this trip; the *Mohave* tied up there no more than half an hour. When we were under way again I left the heat and heavy whiskey smell of the saloon and started down the forward staircase, thinking that I would find a shady place on the cargo deck, as I had yesterday, to sit and pass the morning.

The purser, Mr. Brody, was approaching as I reached the foot of the stairs. "Oh, Mr. Boone," he said, "have you been with Mrs. Todd the past few minutes?"

"No, I haven't. Why do you ask?"

"Well, you're a friend of hers. Seeing as how Mr. Mason said he was a friend of hers, too, I thought the two of you might also be acquainted."

I stiffened. "I don't know anybody named Mason. Who is he?"

"Fellow who came aboard at Dent's Landing," Brody said. "He asked if Mrs. Todd happened to be a passenger, and I—"

"What did he look like?"

"Why, a big man with a red beard . . ."

Mase Todd.

I caught Brody's arm; what he saw in my face made him flinch away from me. "Did you tell him which cabin Mrs. Todd is in?"

"Yes, I did. I saw no harm in that. Mr. Boone, what—"

I let go of him, whirled, and ran up the stairs. There was a cold knot of fear in my stomach, and surrounding it, a white-hot anger directed as much at myself as at Mase Todd. Dent's Landing. The road leading out of the settlement into the desert—the same road I had come to days ago, branching off from El Camino Real del Diablo, with the sign at the fork that spelled out the name Dent's Landing. Damn! I should have remembered that long before now, realized Todd and the yellow-haired man might have split up there. They hadn't known when they reached the fork which direction Jennifer might have gone; Todd had followed the Dent's Landing road, waited at the settlement for the first steamer to arrive . . .

On the cabin deck I ran ahead into the tunnel with my hand on the butt of my holstered pistol. When I neared Jennifer's cabin I forced myself to slow to a walk, eased up next to the door. It was shut. No one else was in the vicinity just then, but I would not have cared if there was; I drew the pistol and leaned up close to the door to listen.

Mase Todd was in there, all right. And so was Jennifer. I could hear their voices coming plain and clear through the louvers.

"Goddamn you, woman!" Todd was saying. His voice was thick with the threat of violence. "I want that money! Now where is it?"

"I told you, I don't know anything about any money—"

"What did you do with it?"

"You've searched the cabin, Mase, you've seen that I don't—"

"You hid it somewhere, or gave it to somebody. You tell me where it is, Jenny, or I swear to Christ I'll kill you right here and now."

Tension and rage made the blood pound in my head. I looked down at the latch. There was no way to tell if Todd had locked it after he'd got inside, but the doors were thin on these cabins and none of the locks was sturdy; it would not take much force to break one loose.

Todd's voice said, "You gave it to that drifter to keep for you—that's it, isn't it? You took up with him after you ran off. He's on board too."

"No! I don't know who you're talking about!"

"The hell you don't. I can see it in your face. Where does he have it? In his cabin?"

"No . . ."

"Tell me, you bitch."

"Oh God, Mase, please don't hurt me . . ."

"I'll hurt you, all right. I'll hurt you plenty."

And he hit her. I could hear the sharp smacking sound of the blow, Jennifer's cry of pain. The rage boiled over in me and I went a little crazy with it. I stepped back a pace, kicked at the door savagely, just above the latch, with the bottom of my boot; the lock splintered free, the door burst open, and I charged inside with my eyes and my head full of a dark red haze.

Jennifer was sprawled sideways on the lower bunk, holding her face where he'd struck her. Todd had been standing over her, bent forward at the waist, but he came wheeling around now, his bearded face flushed with fury and surprise, and went for the weapon holstered on his hip.

"Roy!"

There was no time for me to stop my momentum and bring my .44 up for a shot, no way I would have done that in any event because of the risk of hitting

Jennifer. I barreled into Todd with my left shoulder, sent him reeling backward into the closed door to the deck. He caromed off it, spilled down on his side; his pistol jarred loose and skittered under the bunks.

I stumbled sideways, caught my balance against the washstand. Jennifer cried out again and scrambled off the lower bunk. I yelled at her, "Get out of here, get help!" and as she obeyed, ran out of harm's way into the tunnel, I went after Todd.

He was on his knees, but he didn't try to crawl or lunge for his pistol; he reared up instead. The look of him swelled the hatred inside me. I tried to kick him, foolishly, and he clawed at my leg and half spun me around, off-balance again, over into the side bulkhead. By the time I recovered, he was on his feet and there was a knife in his hand, a big skinning knife with a wicked-looking blade.

He raked at me with it as I came around, and I couldn't dodge clear in time. The blade sliced through my forearm above the wrist, bringing a spurt of blood. The hand went numb; I heard my pistol thump on the deck.

But I was still moving, and he missed me with a second swipe of the knife. I managed to get around the washstand so that it was between us when I faced him again. I saw where my pistol lay, but it was closer to him than it was to me; I couldn't get to it in the face of that knife. And I couldn't get out of the cabin and away from him, either. I stood my ground, breathing in ragged gasps, my right arm hanging bloody and throbbing at my side as Todd straightened again with the knife held out in front of him. There were maybe six feet separating us.

His eyes were wild, vicious; I quit looking at them. You could not defend yourself against a knife by watching anything except the weapon itself. I stayed motionless, waiting. Todd's fingers were loose around the wooden handle; when he made his move the fingers would tighten in reflex an instant early.

I could hear voices and movement out in the tunnel, but it was too soon to expect help from that quarter. Sweat flowed thick and hot under my arms and along my sides. A tic started below my left eye, but I dared not blink. Just that much time might give Todd all the advantage he would need.

The fingers tightened; he made a low sound in his throat and lunged forward with the knife.

I twisted to one side, thrust my hips back, and bowed my body in the middle. The underhand slash cut through the fabric of my shirt, and the knife hung up there briefly before it came free. That gave me enough time to slam my left fist down on his wrist with enough force to dislodge the knife, send it clattering to the deck. Then I threw myself against him and drove him sideways into the bunks.

We reeled off, back into the center of the cabin. I had hold of him by then, crowded in close, the fingers of my left hand bunched in his shirt. He hammered a blow at the side of my head, tried to bring his knee up between my legs. I managed to turn aside, to punch the toe of my boot into his shin, but I couldn't bring him down. He was stronger than I was, and with my right arm cut the way it was, I couldn't hold him either; he broke loose and hit me again, hard over the cheekbone.

The blow knocked me backward, and the back of my head struck the edge of the upper bunk. Black streaks blurred my vision. And I was the one who lost footing, spilled down to one knee.

But Todd didn't come after me this time. I heard more shouts from the tunnel, people milling around out there, and he heard them too. Panic came into his face—I saw it as I pawed my eyes clear—and he pivoted and plunged out through the doorway. Someone grabbed his arm, tried to stop him. Todd twisted free of the man and disappeared aft, running.

I struggled to my feet and went after him, pushing my way through the passengers and crew members clogging the tunnel. Pain and rage and hatred fogged my mind; all I could think of was getting my hands on him again, making him pay in blood for what he'd done to me and all he'd done to Jennifer.

When I came out into daylight Todd was at the aft stairway, flailing at those in his way with both hands. He made it down to the cargo deck, bowled over one of the soldiers, and then ripped the man's sidearm from its holster. Some of the other troopers had started to move in on him, but when he came up waving the pistol and shouting like a madman, they backed off. Somewhere up above, a woman was screaming. If Todd opened fire with that pistol, there would be a mass panic and any number of people would be hurt.

Todd backed off to the starboard rail, still waving the handgun. He saw me come off the last of the stairs, and I could tell by the wildness and hate on his face that he would shoot me if he could. I did not stop, I couldn't have stopped if I had wanted to. I ran straight at him, with my head lowered, and I slammed into him and knocked his arm up just as he squeezed the trigger.

The force of my momentum flung both of us up over the rail and down into the muddy river.

I was above him, clutching at his shirt with my left hand, the echo of the shot and the cries of the passengers like thunder in my ears, when we hit the water. The shock of it constricted my lungs; water poured into my open mouth, my nose. We tumbled over and over, caught in the force of the turbulence created by the *Mohave*'s bucketing paddle wheel, but I did not lose my grip on Todd's shirt.

He thrashed frantically, trying to get clear of me

and up to the surface. Clawed fingers scratched and fumbled at my throat. Then one of his hands caught my jaw, hung on with nails gouging.

I twisted my neck and got free of the grip. My cheek touched the inside of his forearm; I heaved up with my elbow, felt solid impact. But the blow didn't hinder the flailing of Todd's arms, and when the black turbulence swirled us over again we jarred into the shallow, sandy bottom. That and his struggles broke my own hold; in the next second he was gone.

I hadn't taken much breath before we'd gone under; pressure built to a roaring inside my head and lungs, seemed to swell them until they felt ready to burst. In desperation I pulled my legs under me and lunged off the bottom, fought upward through the storming water. As shallow as the river was, I broke surface immediately. I sucked air into my lungs, gasping, shaking my head, and blinking to clear my vision.

The *Mohave*'s passing afterwash spun me around so that it was three or four seconds before I could see either the boat or Todd. He'd come up closer to it than I had, over toward the huge spinning buckets of the paddle wheel, and he was caught in the frothy tumult. His arms lashed the water frenziedly as he struggled to swim clear—but I could see that he was not going to make it. The churning force of the paddles was dragging him backward, pulling him into the wheel.

Then one of the buckets smashed into his head and drove him under, and I heard the screams of the women passengers as the wheel swallowed him.

I was afraid that the same thing would happen to me; I swam hard with the current, downriver. But it was only a few seconds before I was clear of the turbulence, able to struggle toward the Arizona shore. The current was so strong that I had to go under again and drag myself across it sideways along the bottom. By the time I got to where the river was shallow enough so that I could stand and walk out, I was seventy-five yards downstream from the *Mohave*. Captain Mellon had veered her over to the bank by then and shut down the wheel, and the deckhands were shipping anchor and standing by with lines. It would not be long before they came ashore to fetch me.

I sat down on the bank and looked away from Arizona, across the river to California.

CHAPTER 18

JENNIFER AND I left the *Mohave* at Ehrenberg the following day.

Captain Mellon and the purser, Mr. Brody, accompanied us to the Colorado Steam Navigation Company office, where we turned the stolen money over to the agent in charge. I had explained the whole story to the captain, and he relayed it to the agent, who in turn sent a telegraph message to the marshal in Yuma. A downriver steamer was due in two days; Jennifer and I, in the company of the agent, would board it with the money.

Mase Todd's body had not been recovered from the swift-moving waters of the Colorado; there was no way to prove, except by my testimony and Jennifer's, that he and the other two had been the ones who'd robbed the territorial bank in Maricopa Wells. So I expected that we would be detained in Yuma for a time, while the marshal investigated. But the fact that we were voluntarily giving up the stolen money was a strong point in our favor—and Jennifer had already admitted her foolishness in taking the money from the dead man at the ranch, a mistake that the law would surely be willing to forgive. There seemed little doubt that we would be allowed to go on to San Francisco before long.

There was no hotel in Ehrenberg, but the steamship agent offered to put Jennifer up at his home. As for me, I could bunk in the hayloft at the freighting station corral. The arrangements suited us both, and we agreed. The agent locked the money in his safe, then led Jennifer away to put her in the care of his wife.

I said good-bye to Captain Mellon and Mr. Brody at the landing and stayed there until the *Mohave* departed again and vanished around one of the upriver bends. The last glimpse I had of her was that huge bucketing paddle wheel beating the water into white swirls. I thought again, for what I hoped would be the last time, of Mase Todd. He had died as he'd come to live, in a froth of violence—a fitting end to an unfit man.

In the loft at the station corral, I slept through the heat of midday and then lay awake until after six o'clock, coming to terms with myself. Admitting, finally, a decision I had already made. Then I washed up and found my way to the agent's house: He had invited me to take supper with him and his wife and Jennifer and given me directions.

Jennifer was in better spirits tonight than she'd been yesterday and this morning. She had been badly shaken by her husband's appearance on the *Mohave,* by the fight between him and me, and by the circumstances of his death; she'd kept saying afterward, as she helped one of the soldiers bandage my cut arm, how it could have been me instead who'd been dragged into the wheel and killed. It had touched me at the time that the thought of my dying should be so unbearable to her, and it touched me again now that I remembered it. If she felt that way about losing me, I did not want to lose her either.

The four of us ate and made conversation, and the whole time I kept fidgeting, looking mostly at Jennifer, because there were things I had to say to her and they were scratching at my throat to get themselves said. As soon as the meal was finished, I took her aside and asked her to walk with me down by the river. She smiled and said she would.

When she had her shawl we left the house and went at an angle toward the Colorado, away from the landing in the middle of town. Jennifer's hand was on my arm; I felt like a man out courting, and in a way I was.

Neither of us said much until we had left the clustered buildings of Ehrenberg and were walking along the riverbank to the south. It was near sunset, and the sky was painted in red and copper and gold that made the arid land to the west look soft, the way fertile land does even under the noonday sun. I stopped and turned to her, and in that colored light her face was soft, too, and her eyes were the prettiest eyes I'd ever seen.

There was a shyness in them now, and a shyness in me as well as I faced her. But I did not feel awkward or uncertain any longer. Just the shyness and a sweet kind of ache—the same kind I had felt ten years ago in that small Kansas town when I first saw Emma. And a sense of conviction that the decision I had made was the right one.

"All day," I said, "I've been thinking about what you said two nights ago. About how there could be a future for us if I wanted it too."

"And do you want it?"

"Yes. I can't keep on living in the dead past, or trying to run away from it, and I can't deny my feelings for you. The fact is, I . . . well, I . . ."

"It's just a word, Roy. If you feel it, you can say it."

"Can you say it?"

"I love you, Roy Boone," she said.

The words came easy this time, much easier than I had expected they would. "I love you, Jennifer," I said.

She smiled, then leaned up and kissed me gently on the mouth.

Nothing else needed to be said, not just now. Later there would be a great deal to discuss—plans for our marriage, plans for the future—but there was plenty of time for that, just as there was plenty of time for us to learn to know each other. Everything slow, not too much all at once—that was the way it ought to be between a man and a woman.

I took Jennifer's hand and looked out across the river again. The gallows land was behind us now, in more ways than one; we had crossed it and survived it, and the new land that lay ahead for us would be much easier to cross because we would be doing it together. For the first time in four months and eleven days, my life had some meaning again, and I was at peace.

Wherever Emma was, if she knew what was happening, I was sure now that she approved.